Revenge

T.K. Eldridge

Graffridge Publishing

First published by Graffridge Publishing 2019

Copyright © 2019 by T.K. Eldridge

All rights reserved. No part of this publication may be reproduced, stored or transmitted in any form or by any means, electronic, mechanical, photocopying, recording, scanning, or otherwise without written permission from the publisher. It is illegal to copy this book, post it to a website, or distribute it by any other means without permission.

This novel is entirely a work of fiction. The names, characters and incidents portrayed in it are the work of the author's imagination. Any resemblance to actual persons, living or dead, events or localities is entirely coincidental.

T.K. Eldridge asserts the moral right to be identified as the author of this work.

T.K. Eldridge has no responsibility for the persistence or accuracy of URLs for external or third-party Internet Websites referred to in this publication and does not guarantee that any content on such Websites is, or will remain, accurate or appropriate.

Designations used by companies to distinguish their products are often claimed as trademarks. All brand names and product names used in this book and on its cover are trade names, service marks, trademarks and registered trademarks of their respective owners. The publishers and the book are not associated with any product or vendor mentioned in this book. None of the companies referenced within the book have endorsed the book.

Historical facts may have been altered in the creation of this book. (It's fiction, people - have fun with it!)

Cover by Lizzie Dunlap of PixieCovers.com

Editing by Donna A. Martz of MartzProofing.com

To all the dreamers who dream of that 'someday'. Don't quit.

To Elisabeth, Maureen, & Olivia - always my daughters, no matter what.

"What goes around, comes around." - C.S. Eldridge

"The best revenge is a life lived well." (variation on quote by George Herbert)

Contents

1. Chapter 1 — 1
2. Chapter 2 — 11
3. Chapter 3 — 19
4. Chapter 4 — 25
5. Chapter 5 — 37
6. Chapter 6 — 43
7. Chapter 7 — 53
8. Chapter 8 — 61
9. Chapter 9 — 71
10. Chapter 10 — 81
11. Chapter 11 — 95
12. Chapter 12 — 107
13. Chapter 13 — 115
14. Chapter 14 — 125
15. Chapter 15 — 139
16. Chapter 16 — 147
17. Chapter 17 — 155
18. Chapter 18 — 161
19. Chapter 19 — 169
20. Chapter 20 — 177

21.	Chapter 21	183
22.	Epilogue	189
23.	Dead & Buried Sample	193
About the Author		199

Chapter One

Cullen stood barefoot in the circle with some of the most powerful people in the United States. A full moon shone down as they surrounded the figure of the US Vice President, Edmund Matthews.

Beside Edmund stood Mirabelle Legarde, Chief Justice of the Supreme Court. They were here for Lammas, the first harvest festival of the witch's calendar – a celebration of the ripened fruit and grains. It was also a time to strengthen protections against evil, and one of the reasons why they were all here. On one side of Cullen stood his brother, Connor, the leader of the Garda. On the other side stood his fiancée, Emlen, the daughter of the current President of the United States, and publicly known as the fiancée of the Vice President. Edmund's true partner, Patrick, stood beside Emlen. Scattered around the circle were a second Justice of the Supreme Court, the liaison between the United Nations and the International Criminal Court, members of the US Congress, leaders of several Intelligence agencies, and multiple members of law enforcement. Family and friends were also present, including Susan Martin, Emlen's honorary aunt and friend of her late mother, Camille.

Edmund stood in the center, holding a silver bowl filled with jewelry, while Mira held her hands over the bowl. Recharging the protection spells on the pieces all at once was easier on the caster. Using the full circle and full moon energy meant they'd be even more effective. Considering what they were all up against? The additional power would be needed. Cullen knew that John Frederick Jackson, the President of the United States and the true head of the Order of St. Michael, would continue to be a formidable enemy until they took him down.

Once the ceremony ended and the circle opened, people wandered about the space, enjoying fresh-baked bread, wine, and cider. Platters were laid out on several tables, bearing fruit, cheese, and meat. Some took plates and sprawled on the grass while others sat at the tables. Torches and landscape lighting added to the moonlight, making it easy to see. The half-acre far in the back of Mayfield, Edmund and Patrick's Maryland estate, had been walled in with old brick, a few plantings and a wide brick circle path that hid the true purpose of the sacred space. In the center, a star-shaped fountain rose about waist high that, laid over with a board and cloth, made a perfect altar space. Cullen got himself a drink and a plate, taking a seat next to Emlen at one of the tables.

Emlen stopped talking to Mira long enough to lean over and kiss Cullen's cheek. "Hey hon. You doing okay?"

"I'm good. Still absorbing the experience," Cullen replied.

"Your first circle?"

Mira asked, dipping a wedge of apple into warm caramel sauce.

"Yeah. I didn't know it would feel like that. That I'd feel what I did," Cullen stumbled a bit on the words and took a sip of wine before continuing. "It was beautiful and sacred, like watching the priests arrange communion at Mass, but I felt it more. The power rushing through my feet into my whole body."

"You're a witch, Cullen. You're going to feel it, every time. It may not be as intense every time – we've got some seriously powerful people here tonight, but you will feel it," Mira told him.

"It's not just the power," Cullen replied. "I mean, if anyone had told me a year ago that I'd be sitting next to my fiancée, talking to the Chief Justice of the Supreme Court about magic in the Vice President's back yard, I would have arrested them for being a drug user."

Emlen chuckled and even Mira laughed a bit. "Well, nothing like diving into the deep end for you, eh, Cullen?" Mira said.

"I wouldn't have believed the changes in the past year of my life either," Emlen told them.

"Change is coming fast and furious for all of us," Mira said. "Hopefully, we'll make sure those changes are in our favor. Thomas has made great strides with Connor in setting up the Paranormal Law Enforcement Alliance. They've managed to get some of our Intel folks as well as one or two from MI, MI, and Mossad on board."

"Now that's impressive," Emlen said. "I know Connor didn't want to give up his position with the Massachusetts State Police, but ever since the late Cardinal passed the Garda on to him, he hasn't stopped."

"My brother needs faster roller-skates," Cullen teased as the man himself dropped into a seat next to his brother.

"Why do I need roller-skates?" Connor asked, making himself a sandwich out of the offerings on the platter.

"To keep up the insane pace of your lifestyle now," Emlen replied.

"No kidding, huh?" Connor said, taking a huge bite of the sandwich.

"Easy, man, you'll choke," Cullen teased.

"How's it really going, though?" Mira asked Connor.

"Better, now that Thomas has Elisabeth helping. I know he's here tonight, but he's mostly been staying at The Hague while she handles the UN side of things."

"I'm glad she took the job," Mira said. "She has a brilliant legal mind and a gift with diplomacy."

"I'm glad she did, too," Connor replied. "I had started to worry about Thomas being stretched too thin. Basing myself in Boston has made it easier for me to get here or to New York when needed. But I'm no good in the Netherlands and I think Thomas slept only on flights back and forth. Everything's taking shape though. We just need to keep Jackson from finding out and blowing it up."

"Does he have enough pull to do that?" Cullen asked.

"If he influenced the right people, he could screw the whole thing up for a while," Emlen replied. "That telepathy influence thing he does is insidious."

Cullen refilled Em's mug of warm apple cider and slid a couple of brownies in front of her. "I saved you two."

Em smiled at him. "Thanks, luv. I wanted chocolate but I also want to sleep."

Mira watched them both with a smile, then frowned as she gave Em a closer once-over. She leaned close to Emlen and whispered in her ear, then pulled back to look at her face. Emlen paled, grabbed Mira's hand and the two walked away from the table.

Cullen started to rise and Connor tugged on his brother's sleeve. "Women's business, leave it." "But..." Cullen started and Connor cut him off again.

"I said leave it. Em's fine. She'll come back for the brownies, at least," Connor teased his brother. "By the way, congrats on the engagement. Ma and Da are over the moon happy."

Emlen had heard the words Mira whispered to her, the truth she'd been trying to avoid came crashing down. "I can't be. Not now," Em said.

"Unfortunately, timing has never been something babies pay attention to,"

Mira replied. "Did you not know?"

"I suspected, but with everything else going on, I didn't want to think about it."

"Well, now you need to think about it. Any idea how far along you are?"

"No more than six weeks, maybe as few as four. How could you tell?" Emlen asked.

"Your aura, the power around you. It has changed since we first met. A new glow, centered around your belly."

"Okay, so not something the average magical person could detect?"

"No, not many will be able to see it. Maybe three people here tonight, total."

Emlen let out a slow breath. "Good, that means JJ won't be able to tell."

"No, and not any of the lackeys close to him either," Mira said.

"So I have some time."

"With a first, you probably won't even start to show until about six months in, so yes, you have time."

"Well, I guess we have a countdown clock on getting things done – because if JJ finds out I'm pregnant and doesn't believe the child is Edmund's, I'm dead."

"Who are you comfortable with letting in on the secret?" Mira asked.

"Let me tell Cullen first, and then Edmund and the rest. Just the inner circle if you don't mind?"

"Can you tell Cullen tonight so we can let the others know tomorrow at the meeting, before everyone goes back to work?"

"I will tell him tonight," Emlen said, a hand sliding over her belly as a slow smile of wonder lit her face. "Wow, I'm going to be a mom."

Mira laughed and hugged her. "You're going to be an amazing mom, and I'm claiming honorable auntie status right now."

"Auntie? How about godmother and auntie?" Emlen asked, hugging back.

"You've got it, Em. Whatever you need." Mira kissed her forehead and turned to lead her back to the table.

Emlen glanced over at Mira and squeezed her hand. The older woman stood a touch taller than Em, slender and fit with silver white hair in short braid that hung between her shoulders. Dusky skin and bright green eyes showed Mira's Cajun heritage as she settled back in her seat at the table.

Em leaned over and tugged Cullen's hand, "Come walk with me for a moment?"

Mira smiled up at them both and lay a napkin over Emlen's brownies. "I'll protect your dessert. Hurry back."

Cullen rose at Em's tug and they walked towards the section of wall nearest them, out of audible range of anyone. "Are you okay, Em?" he finally asked.

"I'm good. In fact, now that it's starting to sink in, I'm really good," Em replied.

"Now that what is sinking in?"

Emlen bit her lower lip, then said, "I'm pregnant."

Cullen blinked and his gaze went from her face to her belly then back up to her face. "Are you sure?"

Em nodded. "Mira can see the energy difference in my aura. It also explains why I've been so tired the past few weeks. I thought it just from all of the stress and chaos."

Cullen's expression slowly slid into a huge smile. He wrapped his arms around Emlen and kissed her, then spun her in a tight circle before putting her back down.

Her cry of surprised laughter brought the attention of a few their way, but no one came over to interrupt. "I'm going to be a dad!" Cullen said, laughing low. He hugged Em for a moment longer then stepped back a pace as the smile faded. "Oh, wait a minute. Now what do we do?"

Emlen gave a small snort of laughter and replied, "We will be having a baby in about thirty-four weeks. That's what we do. But yeah, I get what you're asking. Mira said we'll have a meeting tomorrow morning with the inner circle and let everyone know so we can discuss moving up the timetable."

Cullen let out a huff of breath. "We need to take care of this so I can marry you before the baby comes."

"We need to take care of this before JJ finds out and tries to kill me," Emlen replied.

"About how…"

"Mira says I have until about six months in, as this is my first, before I start to really show. I can hide it with loose clothes and such as much as possible. If JJ knows I'm pregnant and it's not Edmund's, I'm as good as dead."

Cullen gripped her hand almost too tight. "We won't let anything happen to you or our child. I won't let anything happen to you."

Susan approached the two of them just then and reached out to give Emlen a hug. "Thank you for inviting me tonight. I've missed a true circle celebration." The glow of happiness around her showed the truth in her words.

"I'm so glad you could be here," Emlen replied. "Did I hear you were going to stay with a friend at the coast for a few days?"

"Yes, my friend from college, Angelica, is here. She invited me to her beach cottage. I'll be sure to stop back at Mayfield before heading back to Boston. Thank you again, dear girl," Susan kissed her cheek and then hurried off to catch up to her friend.

Cullen leaned down to kiss her again just as Em's stomach growled. They both burst into laughter.

"I think your son wants brownies," Emlen told him.

"Or your daughter," Cullen teased. "Let's go feed you both."

Chapter Two

The next morning, brunch was served in the conservatory at the back of Mayfield manor. All of the inner circle that were in town had stayed overnight. They gathered around the glass topped table, enjoying the delicious selection set out for them. Edmund and Patrick sat at one end of the large oval with Mira and Thomas at the other. Cullen, Emlen, and Connor sat along one side while Stefan and Kate sat across from them. Emlen had met Kate before but this had been the first time she had a chance to sit down and talk to her. In her late forties, Kate boasted long, thick, dark hair and dark brown eyes. She looked closer to thirty than fifty and tended to use her hands when she spoke. Kate also acted as the Managing Editor for Digital, Photography, and Social Media for the Washington Press, which meant she could help spin anything and everything. Stefan neared Emlen's age, mid-twenties, and while he had the lowliest job title, he also had the most access to Congress. He served as an intern for Edmund's office which also allowed him access to the House and Senate. Running errands, doing research, Stefan had the ability to hear and see things the rest of them would miss. A short cap of blond hair and dark blue eyes, he looked like a skinny kid who thrived on caffeine and running. Stefan was the coven's secret weapon for sure.

Edmund Matthews had been a second term Senator when the team had blackmailed the President into making him his Vice President. That had been a few weeks ago, and he and Patrick, his life partner and Chief of Staff, had moved into the Observatory, the traditional residence for the VP. No one outside the coven group knew that Patrick and Edmund were handfasted – and they were keeping it that way. The public, and the President, were all under the impression that Emlen and Edmund were engaged to be married. Edmund was also the brother of Elise Matthews Jackson, the President's late wife and Emlen's stepmother. Elise had been killed on the Summer Solstice while at Cullen's house in Muckle Cove. The previous head of the Garda, Cardinal Liam McKinsey, had arranged her murder. The President, merely the VP at the time, had known the plan, and also knew Elise had been six months pregnant with his son. A week or so later, Jackson had staged a great cover story by having Emlen visit him at the White House the same day he'd arranged to have a missile hit the Oval Office, killing Hugh Bannerman, the President. It had been that attack that allowed the coven to blackmail Jackson into making Edmund his VP before he had been sworn in. Yet all the evidence they had right now qualified as circumstantial. They needed solid proof to get Jackson out of office and he had so far proved slick enough, powerful enough, to make that a difficult task.

Connor put down his fork and leaned back with his coffee. "So, it has been decided that perhaps our best next move would be to take down Reginald Dunleavy and his cadre at the Order. We know Jackson is the real leader, but with his figurehead disabled, it should cause him some issues."

"I've compiled a few dossiers on the upper echelon of the Order and I'll have them sent to each of you. We should consider building a case to have them all taken down en masse due to corruption and criminal enterprises," Mira said.

"Except that will take a long time, and we don't have a long time," Emlen said. "We need to take down Jackson in the next few months – before I start showing." She reached out and gripped Cullen's hand, then looked back at the rest of the table.

Mira smiled, lifting her orange juice glass in a toast, and then the table erupted with cheers and congratulations. As much as this pregnancy upended their timetable, it was a joyous event to celebrate. Hugs for Emlen, handshakes for Cullen and a lot of chatter derailed the conversation for a few minutes.

Once things settled back down, Kate spoke up. "As to the timetable, that's where I come in. We don't need the proof all lined up and ready for a jury to cause enough public backlash and doubt in his abilities. That may be enough to get Jackson out of office. We'll need the proof to go before a Congressional Committee, but not to get public sentiment against him."

"Basically, trying him in the court of public opinion, right?" Cullen said.

Kate nodded. "Exactly. We have enough friends in Congress that we could get people talking about impeachment, even though without solid proof, we have nothing to act on. The threat may be enough to get him to resign with his dignity intact."

"I may not know my father very well, but I doubt he'd give up power for a little lost dignity," Emlen said.

Edmund nodded. "True, but there is a lot more power in being a resigned President who wasn't elected into the office, than there is in being an impeached President who murdered his way into the office."

Cullen leaned forward, elbows on the table. "So, how can I help?"

"Keep acting as Emlen's Garda. Kian and Micah are around, but they're also helping with overall security at Mayfield. We need someone whose main focus is Em," Connor replied.

"That's great. I will, of course, continue to protect the mother of my child, but I can do more," Cullen said as he turned to the others. "Before all of this, I worked as a contractor and before that, a cop. I have a Bachelor's in Criminal Justice. I'm more than just Em's guard."

"And you've been an amazing help with everything Connor and I have been working on," Thomas told Cullen. "Your input on setting up PLEA has been incredibly beneficial."

"Then let me keep helping with that. Don't get me wrong, I love spending time with Emlen, but while she's writing, training or dealing with her duties here at Mayfield, there's no real need for me. I'm the kind of person who has to feel like I'm contributing my share."

"Let me add, as much as I love having Cullen around, there are times I want my space," Emlen said.

Thomas thought for a minute, then asked Cullen, "How would you feel about reviewing case files? Giving your input on what tactics we should take or angles we should look at?"

Cullen glanced at Emlen, then turned to Thomas. "Sounds good to me. I already know the kind of framework PLEA has in place, so I can work within that and make recommendations."

"I have a question," Em said. "I know PLEA stands for Paranormal Law Enforcement Alliance, but what do you tell non-magical people?"

Connor chuckled. "Pan-global instead of Paranormal. We tell them we recruit and serve worldwide as additional manpower for specific cases brought to us by other law enforcement agencies. Which, to be fair, is true. Just not in the way they would assume."

"People will believe what they want to believe, which is why I spend more time verifying stories than I do writing my own," Kate said.

"And why I stay off social media," Emlen added. "Ever since Elise's funeral, I've either been portrayed as an angel or a whore."

"Yet half of the people who call you one or the other can't pick your photo out of a lineup. However, the general consensus is that you're a sweet girl caught in an unusual situation, trying to make the best of it," Kate said. "The fact that you're living here and not at the White House or the Observatory is playing in your favor."

"Speaking of the Observatory, did you finally get the master suite cleared? I can't believe how many nasty magical surprises Jackson left behind," Stefan asked.

"If not for Emlen and her psychometry gift, and the help of the ghosts, we would have been in a bad way," Patrick said.

"Weakened, confused, susceptible to illness – Jackson really scraped the bottom of the barrel to try and get back at us for blackmailing him."

"I'm sure he's not done trying to get back at you either," Emlen said. "It's not like him to just let something go."

Cullen rested an arm across the back of Emlen's chair. "Spellcasting is not his strength or gift, either. I wonder who he had do them?"

"Dunleavy," Mira replied. "He comes from a long line of spell makers and his gift is in modifying spells on the fly."

"All the more reason to take that bastard down," Edmund said, as he rose from his chair. "Alright, everyone. Read the dossiers from Mira, brainstorm and let's see what we can come up with as a plan of action. Patrick and I need to get back and I'm sure the rest of you have things you need to be doing." He walked over to Emlen and leaned down to kiss her on the top of the head. "Congrats on the baby, Em. Take care of yourself and the next Descendant."

"I will, Edmund," Em murmured. "You take care too."

People started filing out of the room, but Mira stayed seated. "Emlen, a word?"

Em kissed Cullen's cheek and sent him along before turning back to sit near Mira. "Something up?"

"I wanted to talk to you about this alone. I may have found a way to remove the Descendant curse."

"The curse? You mean, being born with magic?"

"No, the curse part. The part where only one child has children. I found an ancient text that spoke of a similar curse and I have been gathering the essential items. Worst case, it does nothing. Best case, your children can each have children and no one will need die or be barren."

"I'm in," Emlen said. "Whatever it takes, I'm in."

"Next full moon is first week of September. We'll try and do it then?"

"Thank you, Mira," Emlen smiled, then leaned in to hug the older woman. "You're a true gift to all of us. Thank you."

"Aww, you're going to make me blush," Mira replied, shaking her head. "I just do what I see is right. I count myself blessed to know you, Emlen Brewster. Your gifts are going to change the world."

Chapter Three

President John Frederick Jackson sat in his temporary office on the second floor of the White House, chair turned away from the desk.

The view out the window allowed him to watch the construction taking place as they rebuilt the section of the West Wing that once held the Oval office. It would again, but not for a few more weeks. Reginald Dunleavy stood on the other side of Jackson's desk, looking out the window as well.

"Impressive amount of damage," Dunleavy said.

"Well, Javelin missiles tend to take out what they're aimed at, right?"

"And then some. At least the structural repairs are done. I get why what happened was necessary, but it seems a shame to damage a national treasure in order to do it."

"Reggie, do shut up. I don't pay you to comment on what I do or how I do it," Jackson said, turning his chair back around to look at the man across from him. "Tell me how is recruiting going?"

Dunleavy eyed the chair next to him, but he'd not been invited to sit, so he shifted his weight and sighed. "It's down. This new organization, PLEA, is offering a better recruitment package."

"Then fix our recruitment package."

"Yeah, we can't afford to match what they're offering."

"Who the hell is behind PLEA anyway? I've found nothing. Shell company after shell company. I heard they were based out of the Hague, but they're not too pleased with me right now. They're not going to give me anything resembling information we can use," Jackson said.

"I'll see what I can find out," Dunleavy said as he headed out of the office.

Once he got outside, he let out a slow breath and cursed. "Fuckers wouldn't piss on you, JJ, if you were on fire. You're just that loved."

The secretary that sat outside Jackson's office choked on her coffee when she heard Dunleavy's words. She lifted her mug to him in a silent toast of agreement before she turned back to her computer. Reggie went down the hall and out of the building, wondering if he could find any way to get himself out of this mess. He'd been tangled up in the Jackson family and Order business since he had been a teen. The Judge recruited him out of juvie and put him through university at Georgetown with a business degree. He worked for the Order from day one and he'd almost married into the Jackson family. A shudder ran through him as he sat in his car, fingers gripping the wheel. He didn't want to get married, but the Judge had ordered it.

Then Tina had run and Simmons, the sick fuck, shot her in the back. He still remembered the look of surprised terror on her face as they slid her into the hole they'd dug. Reggie saw that face often in his nightmares.

The Jackson family well and truly owned him – well, JJ now did. The Judge would never breathe free air again, so that one was off the list. He almost wished he still only dealt with the Judge. As twisted as the old man had been, his son took things to a whole new level. The spell traps he'd had Reggie leave in the Observatory were downright cruel. Not that cruel bothered Reggie much, not when the person deserved it – but Matthews? He didn't deserve it. Yet.

The new BMW he drove handled like a dream. Reggie loved his nice cars – he had six now. This one worked perfectly as a commuter car in DC. Convertible for the days when the weather allowed, nimble for when traffic would try and slow him down. It wasn't until he hit the GW parkway that he noticed the black Hummer on his tail. He changed lanes a few times and it stayed on his rear, getting closer. Reggie cut over to Spout Run parkway and did his best to lose them, but they kept on him. Two car lengths back, then three – the gap between them grew as he hit the Thrifton Hill Park area. That was the last thing Reggie would ever remember.

A fireball spilled across the parkway, causing vehicles to spin and skid as they tried to avoid the wreckage. The black Hummer pulled over as its occupants watched the car burn. Once they were assured no one would walk away, the vehicle turned and took a side road along with the others trying to avoid the scene.

The McLean Psychiatric hospital often housed the rich, the famous, and the spoiled. The staff were used to entitled arrogance from many of their patients and John Cameron Jackson, once a Federal Judge, was no different. He had made few friends during his stay at the facility. No one wanted to be stuck dealing with the Judge, so it surprised the aide on call when Mario had said he'd take the Judge that afternoon. She sure as hell didn't want to deal with the cranky old bastard, not with her boards coming up. The extra study time would be welcome, so she agreed to switch and sat with Mrs. Sanders who never said a word, just stared at the ceiling all day. Jenny told all of this to the police when they came to investigate the sudden death of the Judge from an apparent heart attack. Mario claimed he had been so distraught by the death, that he had to quit.

Before the police could talk to him. Jenny also found it odd that they couldn't find any trace of the nurse's aide named Mario in their employee database, nor did his fingerprints show up in any system.

The phone rang several times before the old man picked it up to answer. "Yes?"

"Commander, it is done. The Judge and Dunleavy are no more," the mechanical voice said.

"Good work. Payment will be wired to the specified account in fifteen minutes." The old man smiled as he hung up the phone. Two down. His beautiful magician, his charge, his sweet angel had been taken much too soon. He would be joining her shortly, so the time to pay his debts had come. Those who had killed her and those who had failed to protect her – they were all going to pay. Every last one of them. He didn't care if they were Garda or Order, they had let his Valentina die and that could never be forgiven. The man now known as Peter Wolfe hit the controls on his chair to bring him closer to the wall of glass and the view of the Mediterranean Sea beyond. The twisted glimpse of his reflection made his stomach churn, so he hit the button that moved the glass out of the way, allowing the salt air to sweep over him. It had taken him years to build his little group.

The Cardinal's betrayal had made it so easy to scoop up the disenfranchised and angry men that made up his band of rogues. Men who were capable of those things Peter had once been able to do. Things that Peter wished he could still do with his own twisted hands. He knew this one thing, however. They should have let him stay dead, all those years ago.

Chapter Four

Emlen and Susan sat next to the pool, enjoying iced tea and sandwiches. Susan had returned to Mayfield after spending a week with Angelica at her coastal cottage on the Maryland shore. "This is so nice," Susan said, stretched out on the recliner, glass of tea in one hand. "It's going to be hectic when I get back to Massachusetts."

"Because you need to make room for Angelica?" Emlen teased.

Susan blushed and nodded. "I'm so happy she'll be coming to live with me for a while. We'll stay in Massachusetts until winter and then move to her place in Maryland through spring. That way neither one of us has to give up our homes and we can stay connected with our families."

"Were you a couple before?"

"We were, sort of. There was a connection back then, but we ignored it as nothing more than good friends because society wasn't as accepting then. We both ended up marrying men and having families."

"And now you can be true to yourselves. That's a wonderful gift," Emlen said. She was seated at the table next to where Susan lay, eating a sandwich and making notes on a pad next to her plate.

"It really is. We get the best of both worlds."

Emlen put the pen down and looked over at her mother's friend. "Susan, would you like to talk to Mom?"

A beaming smile answered Em's question before Susan's words did. "I'd love to." She rose from the recliner and sat in the seat next to Em. "What do I need to do?"

"Just touch me," Emlen replied. Once Susan had laid a hand on Emlen's arm, Em called out "Mom? Can you come visit with us for a moment?"

It took a minute, but soon Camille was standing on the other side of the table from them. She looked as solid and alive as the two seated women.

Susan's voice cracked with emotion as she whispered, "Oh, my gods. Cami...is it really you?"

Camille smiled as she stepped closer to the two seated. "Yes, Suze, it's me. It's so good to see you."

Susan rose from her seat, keeping one hand on Em's shoulder. "C'mere, sister. I need to give you a hug."

Emlen reached up to take Susan's hand and the other woman wrapped her free arm around Camille.

Tears slid down her cheeks as she hugged her friend. "I have felt so guilty for not being there, that night. I..."

"You would have died, too," Camille told Susan, hugging her back. "Instead, you were here to help my baby girl understand more of her heritage. Priceless, my friend."

Emlen used a foot to push a chair out so Camille could sit beside Susan and the two settled in the chairs, facing each other.

Camille gripped Susan's free hand, both of them searching the other's face. "You're beautiful, Susan," Camille said. "Age is wonderful on you."

Susan laughed and shook her head, "It's not as easy as it looks, but I'm enjoying it for now."

Emlen leaned forward, elbows on the table. "Well, now that I have you both here, I have some news." When both turned to look at her, Emlen continued. "Cullen and I are having a baby."

Silence from them both for a heartbeat before both ladies cheered. "Congrats, Emmy," Susan offered, squeezing the hand she held while Cami got up and leaned through the table to hug her daughter.

"Oh, I'm going to be a grandma," Camille whispered into Em's hair. "I'm so happy for you."

"You're both going to be grandma to this baby, as are Simone and Eileen O'Brien," Emlen said, then paused and looked at Susan, "Well, if you want to be?"

"Of course I do," Susan laughed and kissed Em's cheek. "Babies are wonderful."

"How are you feeling?" Camille asked Em. "Tired? Hungry?"

"Tired a lot and I'm eating more than usual, but no weird cravings yet," Em replied. "I still need to see a doctor, but we've scheduled one to come out next week. I don't need to tell you two how much we need to keep this under wraps."

"Yeah, the last thing you need is JJ finding out," Camille said.

"What did you crave when you were pregnant with me?" Emlen asked Camille.

"In the beginning, fresh tomatoes. I'd eat them like apples," Camille said. "Then in the last couple of months, ice cream. Didn't matter the flavor, as long as it was fruit or chocolate with nuts or chocolate bits. Dishes, cones, shakes, I wasn't that particular."

Emlen chuckled. "I'm kind of liking the idea that I can eat all the ice cream I want."

Susan laughed. "I craved berries at first, then popsicles. Red ones, mostly. With my second, I couldn't get enough of pickles and peppers. Pepperoncini and jars of pickles or giardiniera mix were favorites. Of course, that was my daughter. Fiery and tart fits her personality."

Em rubbed a hand over her still-flat belly. "I wonder what traits this little one will have?"

"They'll be brilliant, no matter what, with you and Cullen as parents," Camille said.

"And gorgeous," Susan added. "Both of you are beautiful people, so no ugly babies coming out of that."

"Aww, all babies are cute," Emlen said.

"No, not always," Susan replied.

"My sister has a son that still looks like someone hit him with an ugly stick. Sweet kid, but it was always a challenge to say something positive about him when she asked, 'Isn't my boy adorable?' and I'd be like, 'He's something, alright.'"

All three of them burst into laughter. Emlen reached out to squeeze her mom's hand too. "You're both so precious to me. I sometimes think of this gift as a curse, but right now? Right now, it is truly a blessing."

Camille leaned in and kissed Em's cheek, then Susan kissed her other. "We're the blessed ones, being able to share this with you. I can't wait to tell Angelica. She'll be knitting and crocheting outfits for the next three winters of the child's life."

Camille chuckled, "I had a friend's mother do that when I was pregnant with Emmy. Six sweater sets, bonnets, booties, even a little dress." She paused and turned to Em. "In fact, there's a dark blue storage trunk in the attic in Boston that has all of that stuff in it. You should get Eileen to go through it and see what is still useful."

"Oh, she'd love that. She's been on the boys for a while to settle down so she could have grand-babies."

Scatha swooped in and sat on the edge of the table, wings fluttering. ~There are strangers in the trees. They are armed. Your security has not yet noticed them. Get inside.~

"Susan, get up quickly, we need to get inside," Emlen's words pitched low but her fear could be heard. "Scatha, go tell Cullen."

The bird flew off and Emlen rose from the chair, keeping the table between herself and the trees.

Susan blinked in confusion for a moment as she got to her feet. "What's wrong?"

"Scatha spotted armed men in the trees. We need to get inside."

Camille shimmered, "I'll go look," before she disappeared. The 1800's plantation sat on over a hundred acres of land. Mayfield boasted stables and riding trails, a shooting range, several ponds and the fenced in garden that served as the coven's ritual space. The house itself sat amid gardens and landscaping that covered nearly four acres before ending in forest on two sides with a brick wall in front and a sloping field behind.

Emlen grabbed Susan's arm and crouched low, looking towards the tree line Scatha had flown from. She couldn't tell if the movement in the brush were people or just the wind. "Let's move," she whispered to Susan and the two women crouch walked behind the concrete planters at the edge of the pool's patio. There was a large stretch of open space between those planters and the low brick wall of the kitchen garden near the house. "Okay, Susan, when I say go, we run and drop down behind that wall over there, got it?"

Susan gave Em a nod. "Got it. At least this old lady can do more than hobble."

A tight smile and Em whispered, "One…two…go!" They pushed to their feet, both running for the back of the house and the three-foot brick shield. The crack of gunfire and the ping of the bullets hitting the patio and metal furniture had both crying out. Four shots. Five. They stumbled and fell behind the garden wall as more shots hit the top, showering them with stone dust and bits of brick. Emlen shook as she glanced over to the house, then turned to look at Susan, a grin on her face. "Almost there…" but her voice trailed off.

Susan was laying on her back, a hand pressed to her side, her bright yellow shirt soaked with blood. "Shit," Emlen said, pulling off her own shirt, leaving her in her bikini top and shorts as she pressed the wad of cloth to the wound. "Hang on, Auntie," she told the woman.

Susan nodded, skin pale and sweaty. "Not going anywhere. Gonna see that baby," she whispered. The gunfire had stopped for the moment, which had Emlen terrified they were moving closer. Then she heard gunfire coming from a different direction. Huddling down over Susan, she prayed to whatever Power was listening to keep them safe.

Camille reappeared and gasped when she saw Susan. Then she yelled for Scatha to get Cullen.

A moment later, Cullen raced out the back of the house towards Emlen. "Em, are you hurt?"

"No, Cull. Susan's been shot. Get help."

Cullen gave Susan a faint smile. "Hey lady, I'm going to carry you inside. It's probably going to hurt and I'm sorry about that."

"Mah heeroo," Susan teased, voice faint. When Cullen picked her up, she gave a soft grunt of pain and passed out.

Emlen ran in front of them and pulled the door open, holding it as Cullen stepped inside. She continued the process as they made their way to the clinic room Edmund had set up months ago.

"Did you..." Emlen started to ask and Cullen interrupted her with, "I called Nina. She was out riding and will be here shortly. Let's get her cleaned up. Grab one of those Quix pads and put it over the wound, it'll stop the bleeding."

Emlen stepped to the cart and pulled open drawers until she found the treated gauze pads, peeling one open and pressing it to the wound. They rolled Susan on her side and didn't see an exit wound.

"The bullet is still inside," Emlen said as they pulled off her shoes and cut her shirt free. A clean sheet was drawn up over her legs while betadine wipes cleaned most of the blood away.

Nina strode in and went to the sink to scrub up while Cullen pulled a clean gown from a packet and held it out for Nina. Gloved and gowned, Nina leaned over Susan while Cullen filled her in. "GSW, no exit wound. She isn't on any meds but takes iron, zinc and a multi-vitamin."

Emlen looked up at Cullen, "How do you know that?"

He held up his phone. "I have her medical file here. We have them for everyone that spends time here, just in case."

"Wow," Emlen replied. "A little invasive, but rather useful right now. I never would've thought about that."

"One of the things I came up with after working with the Garda," Cullen told her, then turned to Nina. "Do you need us to help?"

Nina shook her head. "Adam is on his way. Should be here in the next ten. I'll need to get that bullet out and get scans done. He can assist. You two," she turned to look at them, "should go clean up." Then to Em she added "And you need something sweet. Juice or some fruit. Can't have you feeling shocky when you're pregnant."

Cullen slid an arm around Emlen and led her from the room. They headed upstairs to their bedroom and Cullen stopped, wrapped his arms around her and hugged her close. He could feel her trembling in his arms. "We'll be okay, love. We'll be okay."

Emlen hiccupped a breath, arms wound tight around him. "That was too close, Cull. How'd they get so close? Who were they?"

"I don't know yet. Ryan and Kian went after them with a couple of the other Garda and Secret Service. I'll find out after we clean up and I take care of you. You go ahead and shower, and I'll get some clothes out."

Emlen nodded and turned for the bathroom. A few moments later, he heard the shower come on. He looked down at himself and grimaced, then stepped out into the hall to use the other bathroom to wash up before touching their clean clothes. By the time Em came out, clothes were laid out on the bed for her and Cullen had just stepped back into the room, hair wet and dirty clothes in his hand. "I used the hall bath to clean up," Cull told her. "Go ahead and get dressed. I'll get you some juice and meet you downstairs."

Emlen gave him a weak smile and a soft 'thanks' before she picked up the clothes and retreated to the bathroom once more.

Em made her way down the stairs to the kitchen where she slid onto a stool at the counter. Cullen sat a large glass of orange juice in front of her, then went about the process to fix her an iced latte. Emlen sipped the juice, then broke the silence. "Any news? Anything?"

"Kian and Ryan are questioning two of the men. The rest of the crew is on cleanup. Nina and Adam are still working on Susan."

Em finished the juice and slid the glass back before she rested, arms folded on the counter. "Cleanup means the rest are dead or escaped, right?"

Cullen nodded.

"Should we call an ambulance for Susan? Get her to a real hospital? I mean, I know Nina is an Army trauma surgeon, but aren't we taking a chance with someone's life?"

Cullen put the drink in front of Em and leaned over to kiss her forehead. "Nina is one of the best, and Susan didn't want to go to the hospital. Gunshot wounds must be reported to the police and she doesn't need that headache. If Nina and Adam can't handle it, they will be the first to call for transport. Take a breath, sip your drink and talk to Scatha. He probably has more intel than I do right now."

Emlen reached up to kiss his cheek, took her drink and went to the conservatory room. She stayed closer to the inner wall, dragging a chair over and settling behind the larger potted plants. All of the house windows were reinforced glass but Em still didn't feel safe enough to expose herself that much. 'Scatha, come to me,' she thought and then leaned back to wait.

It didn't take long before Scatha was swooping through the wall and landing on the arm of Em's chair. ~You rang?~

Emlen snorted a laugh at his comment. "Yeah, I did. I was wondering if you had any information on the shooters."

~There were eight total. Two captured, two ran and the other four are dead. I believe Ryan recognized three of them, two of the dead and one of the captured. They were Garda under the Cardinal.~

Em sucked in a breath. "Shit. Anything else?"

~I heard one of the runners say that two out of three wasn't bad, so there were apparently two other attacks today. Successful attacks.~

"I need to tell Cullen," Emlen got to her feet but stopped to look back at Scatha. "If you hear or see anything, please let me know. Susan was still in surgery last I checked and I don't want anyone else getting hurt. Thank you, Scatha."

~I will do my best, Emlen. I'm only sorry I didn't notice them sooner to get you and Susan to safety.~

"That's not on you, my friend. If not for you, we'd both be dead. You're a hero in this, Scatha. Don't forget it." Emlen left the room to find Cullen as Scatha phased through the glass ceiling and into another patrol round.

Chapter Five

Kathy, the President's secretary, opened the door to the President's office and took a step back as a Secret Service agent led two Virginia State Police into the room. Jackson looked up from the papers on his desk and frowned. "What is the meaning of this?"

"Mr. President," the Secret Service agent said, "These two officers need to speak with you about Reginald Dunleavy." The agent then stepped back and stood to the side of the desk.

Jackson rose and leaned his hands on his desk as he looked at the officers. "And what do you need to tell me about Reggie? Did he get a parking ticket?" Sarcasm and attitude dripped from his words as if the officers in front of him had a bag of dog shit to hand over. The older of the two officers lifted his chin, eyes glinting as he held his hat in front of his belt.

"Mr. President," his tone icily respectful, "Mr. Dunleavy was killed today when his car exploded on the Spout Run Parkway."

Jackson dropped into his seat and stared at the officer. "How?"

"We're still determining that, sir. Witnesses say he was speeding down the parkway, weaving through traffic when it exploded."

"Are you sure it's Reggie?"

"Preliminary autopsy results and traffic cameras placing him in the vehicle minutes before the explosion would lead us to believe it is Mr. Dunleavy."

JJ swallowed the sudden lump in his throat, then nodded to the two officers. "Thank you for letting me know. I'd like to see the report when your investigation is done. If you need any assistance, ask my agent for the proper contacts." The Secret Service agent gestured to the door and the two officers turned and left.

Kathy stepped into the open door and asked, "Mr. President, is there anything I can get for you?"

"No, Kathy. Thank you," JJ replied. He reached into a bottom drawer and pulled out a bottle of vodka and a glass, then poured about two fingers worth before tossing it back. He had been refilling the glass when a very pale Kathy opened the door again. "Mr. President."

JJ looked up at her and his brow furrowed at the expression on her face. "What is it, Kathy?"

"Th-there's a call for you on line two. It's the McLean facility." JJ sighed and grabbed the phone then hit the button to connect the call as Kathy stepped out and shut the door.

"President Jackson," he said into the phone. "Mr. President, this is Lawson Gaines, head of the McLean facility. I'm calling about your father, Judge John Cameron Jackson."

"Yes, yes, I know my father is there. What's going on?"

"I'm sorry, Mr. President, but I regret to inform you that Judge Jackson died this morning of an apparent heart attack."

JJ didn't speak and Gaines waited a minute or two before he spoke again. "Mr. President, are you still there?"

"Yes," JJ said, voice rough. "Has there been an autopsy yet?"

"Yes, sir. It's how we determined he had a heart attack. His body is being transferred to Morton's Funeral Home per the instructions he had on file here. If you wish different arrangements, you will need to speak with his lawyer."

"No, that's fine. Thank you for calling," JJ hung up the phone. He glanced at the still-filled glass in his other hand, lifted it, and drained it. Then he threw the fine crystal tumbler against the wall and watched it shatter. The agent outside the door darted into the room, gun drawn.

When he saw JJ leaned back in his chair, both hands over his face, he stopped. "Mr. President, are you injured?"

"No. Get out."

"Mr. President..."

JJ's voice rose and he shouted, "I said, get out! You're fired, you incompetent ass. You can't even listen to simple instructions. Get out, get out, get out!" As he shouted, he pushed to his feet and stalked closer and closer to the agent, backing the man out of the room before he slammed the door. He stomped over to the desk, grabbed the phone and called his Chief of Staff. "Thompson! I want the agent outside my door fired. That idiot Kathy, too. They can't understand basic instructions. Do it now."

The phone was slammed back down without letting the other man speak. His feet carried him back and forth across the room, his fingers twisted in his hair. "My father is dead. Reggie is dead. I know the Garda didn't do it because they don't exist any longer. Who the fuck is after me now?"

A hesitant tap on the door and then a slip of paper slid underneath. JJ tugged the paper the rest of the way clear of the door and opened the note. It was from his secretary, Kathy.

'I'm sorry for your losses today, Mr. President. There is a blackberry pie in the fridge at your coffee bar that I made last night for you. It has been an honor serving you, sir.'

Now JJ felt like a real shitty person. It had been a long time since someone had bothered doing something nice for him, and here she'd gone and made him a pie. His favorite too.

He tugged the door open and called out, "Kathy? Come in here, please."

A moment later, the woman stepped up to the doorway and set a box down just outside of it. A security guard stood behind her. Her face flushed, brown hair streaked with gray twisted into a bun and a neat skirt suit that hid curves and hips well-suited to a late-forties aged woman.

"Yes, Mr. President?"

JJ took a deep breath and let it out. "I was an ass and I apologize. I wasn't myself. Please, stay and continue working for me?"

Kathy sniffled, then gave him a nod. "Of course, Mr. President. But I won't be abused by you again."

JJ's fingers curled into a fist behind his back and he gave her a tight smile. Power oozed from him as he spoke the words. "You will work for me until I no longer need you and you will find it the most fulfilling job you've ever held." He watched her face as the suggestion sank deep into her mind and then smiled. "You said there was pie?"

Chapter Six

"In other news, the President has, once again, fired several members of his staff without cause. This makes a total of thirty-seven people since he took the oath of office. Members of Congress have floated a bill to request the President get a psychiatric work up to eliminate the possibility of illness or disease." Emlen rolled her eyes as the newscaster spoke of her father's increasingly erratic behavior. The TV offered some background noise other than the hisses and beeps from equipment around Susan's bed. Angelica had taken a break to go eat and nap. She'd been sitting by Susan's bed for two days, after Emlen called her the evening after Susan came out of surgery and was considered stable.

Camille shimmered into solid form and rested a hand on Em's shoulder. "You need to rest too, Emmy. Susan's going to be fine. Nina and Adam have been using typical medicine and magic and she's already healed as if it had been a week ago."

"I know, Mom," Emlen replied. "They've both told me she's strong and doing well. I'll believe it when she's awake for more than fifteen minutes at a stretch." Em reached up to squeeze her mom's hand. "Joel came by earlier. I've got to sit with Cullen later so Joel can talk to him. Simone hasn't been around in weeks and Tina is supposed to be spending most of her time at the White House, keeping an eye on JJ."

Camille squeezed back. "I think Simone is hoping she'll cross over but won't until this mess with JJ is settled somehow."

"I know I'm lucky to be able to talk to ghosts, and the fact that I can touch the living and they can see the dead has been beyond helpful for Cullen and Connor. Having Joel's wisdom and input is priceless. But I worry. What if the baby gets this gift? How do I teach a small child to keep magic a secret?"

"I wish I could help you there, Em. I had blocked your magic before you were a year old, so we never really had to deal with it."

"And I understand why you did it. If I didn't have the coven and PLEA around to protect and teach, I'd be considering it too. It's hard enough teaching a child, never mind a magical one." "You'll do fine, Emmy. You have good instincts and a lot of love. That's all you need to start being a parent. The rest comes with experience."

Em reached out to hug her mother and sighed. "I love you, Mom. I'm so lucky to get to know you and spend time with you. But know this," she pulled back to meet Camille's gaze, "if you decide you're ready to move on, let me say goodbye and then go. Don't hang around just because you feel guilty or something, okay?"

Camille cupped Em's cheek and gave her a warm smile. "I promise, daughter. I will say goodbye when I'm ready to go – but that won't be for some time yet."

A choked sound from the other side of Susan's bed had both women turning to look. Tina appeared, looking frantic. "Holy shitballs, you guys are not going to believe what's happened. Wait, what happened here?"

"Susan was shot two days ago. Some guys showed up and tried to kill me," Emlen said.

"Well, that makes my news even more interesting. Reginald Dunleavy died in a car explosion a couple of hours after Judge Jackson died of an apparent heart attack. Two days ago," Tina replied.

"And you're just telling us now?" Camille said.

"Well, I drained my energy staying around JJ for days on end and when I got enough to come back, I heard the news and came right here. I didn't know so much time had passed."

"It's okay, Auntie. You told us as soon as you could. Let's go tell Cullen so he can get the wheels turning with PLEA and the local crew," Em said.

A glance back at Susan to make sure she was still asleep and Em stepped from the room. Emlen found Cullen in what they were all calling the control room. It had been a spare, ground floor bedroom but they needed a space for all of the computer equipment and monitoring screens, so it had been converted. Two of the other PLEA workers were plugged into headsets and staring at monitors, so Em waved Cullen over.

He came out into the hall and when Em took his hand, he stuttered to a stop. "Camille, Tina. Uh...hi?"

"Tina's got something to tell you, Cull. She just came and found me while I had been chatting with Mom."

Tina turned to Cullen and took a breath. "Judge Jackson died from an apparent heart attack at McLean and an hour or two later, Reginald Dunleavy's car blew up on Spout Run parkway with him in it. JJ freaked out and fired half his staff, then rehired his secretary back after doing his brain-goo trick on her. The deaths were two days ago, the same day Susan got shot, I guess. I just found out today because I overdid it and had to recharge. I'm sorry."

Cullen reached out and lightly gripped Tina's shoulder. "It's fine. You told us as soon as you knew and that's all anyone could ask. We had been hearing chatter that Dunleavy had gone AWOL but hadn't put it all together. The Judge's death has been kept out of the media completely. Has JJ said anything useful about either?"

Tina shook her head. "Not really. He rants a lot about Reggie bailing on him when he needed him most. He goes back and forth about whether the Garda did it or some other enemy he has yet to identify."

"Well, if the same people that went after them are the ones that went after Susan and Emlen, they were Garda but didn't take the employment options Connor offered and went their own ways," Cullen said.

Emlen bit her lip, then offered, "Sounds like a rogue group. Someone that didn't like the Garda being dismantled? Someone that has a grievance with what is now PLEA and the Order?"

"If that's the case, then we're going to need to go over every personnel file for those that didn't move on to PLEA or the other groups Connor arranged hires with. I'll get them loaded on a laptop and you can help from wherever you want to be," Cull told Emlen. "I know you're still spending a lot of time with Susan while she sleeps. Cross referencing files won't disturb her, and I'm really going to need your help with this one."

"That sounds fine. I want to help as long as I can be there when she needs me."

Camille touched Em's shoulder. "I'm going to go back and keep an eye on Suze. I'll let you know if she wakes up before you or Angelica get back."

"Thanks, Mom. I'll get back there as soon as I get set up."

Cullen turned to Tina. "Can you give Em a list of those who he's fired and any possible reason you might have heard about for those firings? If it's just JJ going off the rails, that's one thing – but if there's a method to his madness, we need to figure it out before anyone else does."

"Sure, I can do that. I'll fade out until you call me back so I don't burn out again," Tina told Em and slipped away.

Emlen turned her whole body and pressed up against Cullen. "Kiss me while we're still alone for a few minutes. I need to remember how you feel."

Cullen chuckled as he wrapped his arms around her, pulling her tightly to him. He leaned down and brushed his lips against hers, then deepened the kiss. For a few moments, nothing existed but the two of them and the kisses that made Emlen's whole body come alive. The sound of someone clearing their throat by the control room's doorway had them pulling apart and laughing.

Jim, one of the techs working with Cullen, grinned at them as he spoke. "Sorry to interrupt, sir, but Connor is on the vid cam and wants to speak to you."

"Good, we can catch him up on the latest intel. Thanks, Jim," Cullen replied. "Time to get back to work,"

Emlen sighed. "Pick this up later?"

"Where we left off," Cullen said and led her into the room. They settled in front of the monitor and camera, Emlen and Cullen sitting side by side in Maryland with Connor in front of his system in Massachusetts.

"Hey, you two. Sorry to interrupt your day," Connor said.

"Naw, it's fine. We needed to update you on some intel anyway. How's Ma and Da?" Cullen asked.

"They're doing great. Da has taught Barnabas to 'ask' for treats after dinner. It's funny until he decides he wants treats at 4 am, but that's a cat for you."

Emlen laughed. "Sounds like they're a match made in heaven."

"How're you doing, Mama-to-be?"

"Doing good. Eating healthy and no more queasiness for now. Hopefully that's all I'll have to deal with."

"So, what did you need, Connor?" Cullen asked.

"Well, we've been getting reports of attacks on both ex-Garda and Order agents and it's starting to sound like they might be linked."

"Tina told us that JJ thinks a new group has sprung up to go after the old Garda and current Order," Emlen said.

"With the deaths of the Judge and Dunleavy on the same day they hit us here, and with the shreds of information we've managed to get from our captives, it's looking like someone scooped up the disgruntled Garda members who didn't take your offers of employment and sent them after all of us."

"That's what we're thinking, too," Connor replied.

Cullen reached for a laptop and started typing. "I'm setting up a file of all of the personnel records from the Garda for Em to go through. Any that are not currently working for us or truly retired are going to need to be investigated."

"I've got a list I pulled together, it might help narrow down the field," Connor said.

"Soon as Cullen's done, I'll get started," Emlen said and smiled at Connor. "Give Ma and Da my love and tell Ma I said thanks for the goody basket she sent me. I'll catch up with you later."

"Later, Em," Cullen replied as she stood and took the laptop from Cullen. Em leaned down and gave Cullen a quick kiss before she made her way back up to Susan's room.

Cami stood by the window while Susan slept behind her. She turned when Emlen came into the room and kept her voice low. "She's been asleep the whole time. Nina checked her vitals and said she's healing well."

"Thanks, Mom. Connor called in while we were down there, so we talked for a moment. He's been getting other reports about ex-Garda attacking Garda and Order agents. Looks like we've got a rogue faction being funded by someone – but no idea of whom yet."

"What are you going to do?"

"I'm going to go through the personnel files of all of the agents that left the Garda but didn't simply retire or take one of Connor's job offers. Connor also has a list that might help narrow it down, but I'll be researching each person to see where they went after they left."

Camille glanced out the window again. "When Angelica gets back, can we take a break and go for a walk in the gardens?"

Emlen sensed the longing and reached out to hug her mom. "Sure. It'd be good for me, too. We'll take the cart to the walled garden and walk there, it's safer."

Cami smiled and hugged Em back, attention once more on the view.

Emlen settled at the little table with her laptop and started sorting. About half an hour had passed when Angelica came back, looking rested and refreshed. "Thank you, Em. I needed a break. Took a nap, a shower, got food and a short walk outside. I've got a new book loaded on my tablet and my knitting to keep me occupied. Nina filled me in a minute ago, so you go do what you need."

Emlen stretched and closed the laptop, then gave Angelica a quick hug. "Glad you feel better. Sounds like Susan will be up and around in a day or so. I'll give you a break anytime."

Angelica's fingers curled around Susan's limp hand. "She's a fighter, my love. We'll get to live those dreams we've planned soon enough."

Em smiled, laptop under her arm as she stepped out of the room. Cami met her in the hallway and they headed up to the suite. "I want to drop this off and let the guards know I want to go out. They'll have to go with us, but after the attack, I'm fine with that."

"I'm glad you're being smart about staying safe," Camille said.

"I've got to stay safe for more than just me," Em replied, a hand resting on her belly. "I forget, sometimes. I don't feel a whole lot different, so it's hard to remember."

"That'll change," Camille laughed and mimed a huge belly as she waddled.

"Mooom!" Emlen laughed. "That's mean." The two laughed as they headed out to catch the guards and take their walk.

Chapter Seven

The table in the conservatory was set for a casual dinner for six. Edmund, Patrick, Emlen, Cullen, Susan, and Angelica were all being treated to paella, rice, fried plantains, and a light salad. Because Em couldn't partake and Susan was still on pain medication, they'd settled for iced tea and sparkling water instead of wine. Conversation was light and fun, everyone enjoying being together and with their loves on a beautiful late summer evening. When the coffee flan, ice cream, and cups of coffee were served and the staff left them alone, the conversation changed.

Cullen cleared his throat and looked around the room. "I'm glad you're all here tonight, because I wanted to propose something."

"Hey, no more proposing. I already said yes," Em said and everyone laughed.

"That's just it," Cullen replied. "I want to openly be your fiancé. In fact, I want to openly be your husband. I want us to get married sometime in the next month or two."

"Wait...what?" Emlen stared at him. "But we..."

"We can," Cullen said. "Let me explain. The reason JJ wanted you with Edmund was mainly for the bloodlines, yes? Well, we now know I have a Bradford bloodline. You're already carrying my child. It's time he heard the truth and accepted the fact that we're together."

"He has a point," Edmund said. "And let me add that Patrick and I have been talking as well. It isn't right that we're hiding who we are, either. It's time the country came to the realization that not everyone is straight. I'm not ashamed of who I am or whom I love. But I'm acting like I am. That's not right."

Patrick reached up and squeezed Edmund's hand. "I know it will be hard, but nothing worth having is easy. He's already the VP, so it's not like they can do much. They've got their hands full with JJ's crazy antics."

"I think Angelica and I are a perfect example of why none of you should wait. We almost lost our chance to share our love," Susan said as she lifted Angelica's hand to kiss her fingers. "Time is precious and not promised to any of us." Her gaze shifted to take in Emlen and Cullen. "You should get married in the Rose Garden. You are the President's daughter." Then her smile broadened and a dimple flashed. "Make it a double wedding. They won't dare not cover the nuptials of the Vice President then."

Laughter slowly started to build as Angelica added, "Set new precedents, my loves. Shout your love from the rooftops. Don't let anyone tell you no."

Emlen turned to Cullen. "I think that's a great idea. Edmund, can you get an appointment for you, me, Cullen and JJ in the next couple of days?"

"Sure, it'll have to be soon, though. He's supposed to fly to Spain for a summit in a couple of days."

"Excellent. Well," Em's smile grew. "Guess I'll be able to avoid a maternity wedding gown after all."

"What kind of gown do you like?" Angelica asked. "I've always dreamed of wearing my great-great-grandmother Brewster's gown. It's from the late 1800's and has been preserved and stored."

"Oh, that sounds incredible," Susan replied. She was clearly feeling better as her eyes shone with excitement. "I used to work as a seamstress when I was younger, before I transitioned to jewelry work. If you need any alterations or anything, I'd be happy to take a look."

"Thank you, Susan," Emlen said. "I think it might need a few adjustments, but she was short, like me, and we are built similar, so it shouldn't be too much."

Edmund put down his phone and raised his glass. "Tomorrow morning at ten, we will meet with Jackson and clear up the relationships. If we can agree, then we'll do back to back weddings in the Rose Garden of the White House in about six weeks. That will put it just before the G20 summit in Dublin."

Cullen raised his glass. "Sounds perfect. There's a Garda house that Connor kept on the edge of Dublin that we can stay in." He turned to Emlen, "Then we'll find some time to visit the other property on Galway Bay and have a more private honeymoon. Agreed?"

Emlen and Patrick both lifted their glasses and toasted their partners. "Agreed."

At ten the next morning, the four coven members sat in an elegantly appointed conference room where a coffee service, fruit, and a selection of pastries were set out. Em nibbled on a pastry and sipped her coffee, wondering just how long her father would make them wait. Cullen tapped on his phone, then set it to record and flipped it over when JJ walked into the room. Edmund and Patrick had been chatting quietly but fell silent as all four rose to their feet. None of them may have respect for Jackson himself, but they all respected the office of the President.

Jackson sat at the table with the rest of them and poured himself some coffee. One agent stood inside the door, the other outside. "So, to what do I owe the honor of this visit? All four of you, it must be something serious," he said.

"To be honest, it's joyful news. You may not like it, but we've already scheduled a press conference for after this meeting," Edmund said.

Emlen shifted the smirk on her face to a smile and widened her eyes. "You're going to be a grandfather." She'd timed it just right so JJ ended up choking on the mouthful of coffee he'd just taken.

"Well, Edmund, I see you didn't waste any time," JJ said after a moment.

"It's not Edmund's. It's mine," Cullen said. Silence met the statement as JJ's face turned a distinctive shade of red.

"I don't even like women, as you well know," Edmund said. "Patrick and I are partners."

"But..." JJ started to speak.

"I'm of the Bradford bloodline," Cullen said.

"Ohh," JJ replied. "Well then."

Emlen snorted at him and shook her head. "A little obvious, don't you think, Father?"

"We are planning back-to-back weddings in the Rose Garden for October twenty-first," Edmund said. "Emlen and Cullen, then Patrick and I. We're announcing it at the news conference in fifteen minutes."

"And if I don't approve?" JJ said.

"Not up to you," Emlen replied. "Imagine how it would look if the President's daughter and the Vice President weren't allowed to use the Rose Garden for their weddings because the President didn't approve? I daresay the public response would not be something you would appreciate."

JJ snarled and slapped his hand on the table. "How dare you."

Emlen gave him a saccharine smile. "I dare because you don't. You don't dare push back because we have all of that proof about Bannerman's murder."

JJ rose to his feet and trembled with fury. "You little bitch."

Emlen reached out and grabbed his arm. "Tina would like to talk to you."

JJ started to jerk his arm out of her grip, then froze as he saw his dead sister standing behind Emlen, as solid as any other person in the room and about as angry as he'd ever seen her. His face paled and he dropped back into his seat. "How?"

"Shut up, John. You're acting like a total dick," Tina said.

"But, you're dead," JJ said.

"No shit, Sherlock," Tina replied. "And you're not, but whatever goodness was in you is most certainly dead." She walked closer and reached out to touch his face, and it caused him to flinch back. Tina paused, then cupped his cheek. "John, you're doing exactly what Father did to me, to your daughter. That's unacceptable."

JJ's hand lifted to press against Tina's hand where it lay against his face. "Vali, what happened to you?"

Tina's expression softened with the childhood nickname and she sighed. "Father tried to marry me off to Reggie and when I tried to run away, Keith Simmons shot me in the back. They buried me in the forest near the Vienna estate. Father told them if I refused to marry Reg, to kill me."

JJ visibly flinched and closed his eyes. "Now you're trying to force Emmy to marry someone she doesn't love. That's not cool, Johnny. Not even a little bit," Tina told him. "Father's gone, Reggie's gone, and you went and gave power to Keith. You need to fix that, and you need to fix this. Let someone in this family find happiness, even if it is too late for us."

JJ nodded. "You're right. At least the guy she chose has a witch bloodline."

"Fuck the bloodline, Johnny. The guy she chose loves her, cherishes her, and treats her like a goddess. That, my dear baby brother, is what is important. Be a better father to Emlen than our father was to us."

"I'll try, Vali. I'll try."

"I need to go. This burns a lot of energy. But, Johnny?"

"Yeah, Vali?"

"I'll be watching you. I have been watching you. Don't be a dick." And with those parting words, Tina faded away.

Emlen lifted her hand from his arm and sat back, watching JJ as his hands lifted to cover his face, then scrubbed at it before he turned to look at them. "I don't know how you did that," JJ said. "But if you drugged me..."

"Oh, for fucks sake, JJ, get over yourself. You're not the only one in the room with power. I've been seeing ghosts for ages and only a few months ago figured out that if I touch someone, they can see them too," Emlen snapped. "It's not all about you, y'know."

"Em, we need to go outside. The press are waiting," Edmund said. The two couples got to their feet and started for the door.

"Wait," JJ said, as he slowly stood. "I'll come with you. I agree and support you in this."

Emlen squeezed Cullen's hand as they all walked out of the room, the agents following behind. She glanced up at the agent that had been standing inside the room the whole time and he looked a little wide-eyed but kept his silence. What was he going to say? He saw the President talking to an invisible person?

Chapter Eight

Keith Simmons rocked the leather desk chair and ran his hands over the polished wood desk. Finally, he had what he believed he had always deserved – the power and prestige of Commander of the Order. Granted, he knew that Jackson truly ran things, but his face was the one the people would see when he sat at the head of the council.

He'd even splurged and bought three bespoke suits for the occasion. Here he was, a little over forty years old, and head of one of the most powerful organizations in the world. Not bad, he mused, for a kid from the streets.

The phone rang and he hit the button. "Yes?"

"Simmons. Is everything arranged for the annual meeting?" Jackson's voice rang out into the room.

"Yes, sir. Oglivy is the only one not attending. He's still recovering from surgery. He'll video conference in from London."

"Fine. The old geezer is nearly ninety anyway. I'll be conferencing in myself. The logistics of getting there and keeping it a secret are impossible for me now."

"Understood, sir. Is there anything else?"

"Watch your tone, Simmons." Keith gulped, then replied more meekly, "Yes, sir."

"Oh, I heard something interesting the other day," Jackson said. "I heard that you were the one that shot my sister in the back in Vienna." Keith stared at the phone and his whole body trembled. "Simmons?"

"Yes, sir?"

"Is that true?"

"Why would I have done something like that?"

"Because my father ordered you to?"

"I would have said something to you by now, if that were true, sir."

"Uh huh. Don't be late tomorrow. It wouldn't look good to have the so-called leader late to his own event."

"I'll make you proud, sir."

"You do that."

The sound of Jackson hanging up the phone had Keith nearly wetting himself. He jerked to his feet and went to the cabinet. His hands shook so hard he slopped the whiskey into the glass and onto the tray beneath. The glass clacked against his teeth as he swallowed the costly liquor and closed his eyes. Jackson was going to kill him. He just knew it.

Peter Wolfe watched the bank of monitors in front of him. Nine screens displayed several camera angles of the inside and outside of the grand hall where the Order gathered for their annual meeting. Behind him, the room was filled with boxes and crates, ready to be shipped to Dublin. After tonight, he would be leaving the Mediterranean for Ireland and the next phase of his plan. After tonight, his beloved's killers would all be dead. Peter sipped juice through a long straw clipped to his shoulder.

He watched the cameras as one hundred and fifteen of the world's most powerful members of the secret society entered the building. The Order of St. Michael had been in existence for centuries. Yet, after today if all went as planned, it would be ended. The camera strapped to Amir was the one he watched the most. It showed him standing off to the side of the hall, facing into the room as the guests took their seats. Tables covered with linen and fine china, flower arrangements, and crystal glasses of wine were set in a large oval. Other cameras picked up the white-jacketed waiter, hands folded in front of him. When Peter saw Keith Simmons enter and take a seat at the table at the peak of the oval, he leaned over and spoke into the microphone.

"As soon as the doors are shut, that will signal that all have arrived. Make your move then." Amir didn't speak, he simply nodded at the instructions. Four other agents were in the room with Amir, and as the doors were being closed, they made their way to the emergency exits. Once outside, they pulled chains from around their waists and proceeded to thread them through the door handles, fastening them with padlocks. One by one, they jogged away from the building and into the darkness.

"As soon as you complete your mission, Amir, I will transfer the funds. May the gods bless you." Peter said into the mic, then leaned back.

Other waiters began moving among the tables, pouring wine, placing salads before the guests, and taking final requests. Amir waited.

Once most of the staff had moved into the kitchens, he stepped towards the center of the oval and faced Simmons. A short bow was offered to the leader who looked at the man in confusion. Amir gave Simmons a faint smile and pressed the switch hidden in his hand. The cameras inside the hall all went black while the cameras outside the hall filmed the explosion that blew out the walls and collapsed the roof of the building. Peter smiled, then reached over and hit a button, transferring two million dollars to Amir's family in Michigan. He saved the video file and leaned back to watch as people came running out of nearby buildings, then as the first responders raced to the scene. There would be no survivors other than perhaps some of the kitchen staff far from the event space. Peter felt a little pang of sadness for the innocents that were involved, but it couldn't be helped. Sometimes innocent blood had to be shed for the greater good. He fell asleep in his motorized chair, watching the screens.

Three days later, Jackson went over the reports again as he listened to one of his intelligence directors explain that they'd found cameras transmitting from around the blast site. The location couldn't be tracked as it had bounced from server to server all over the globe. They were puzzled as to why no one had come forward and claimed responsibility for the bombing that left all but five event staff dead in the E Street attack. The remains of the bomber could not be identified, other than that he was possibly of Middle Eastern descent. Even that they could not be confident about and hoped that forensics would give them more clues.

He dismissed them and turned to look out the windows at the Rose Garden. It was a relief to finally be sitting in the Oval Office at last, but that relief had been short-lived. His whole organization was gone. He had a few thousand foot soldiers left, but no one to pick up the reins of leadership. Even those soldiers were melting away, taking other jobs or retiring. Some had helped themselves to the resources of their local bases before disappearing. JJ had had to scramble to find people to secure the facilities and lock it all down. He had missed seeing the explosion live as he hadn't been planning on teleconferencing in until after the dinner. At least none of the feeds would track back to the White House and cause him even more issues. PLEA had already threatened to take over the facilities and round up any agents they could find, claiming a terrorist threat risk scenario. JJ couldn't help but think that might be the easiest solution. He didn't have time to deal with the Order chaos on top of being President.

"Tina, if you're here, I want to talk to you," JJ said. "I know I can't see or hear you without Emlen, but I really need someone who is on my side."

Silence met his words. "I don't know what to do, sis. I could really use some advice." The room was still silent. "Goddammit, Valentina! Tell me what to do," he shouted. The door flew open and the Secret Service agent scanned the room, looking for whatever threat had the President screaming.

"Sir?" he finally asked, seeing that the room only held Jackson. "Are you in distress?"

"Of course I'm in distress! I want to talk to my goddamned sister and she won't answer me!"

The agent's eyes went wide and he took a step back. "Understood, sir. Shall I send for Dr. Willoughby?"

"I don't need a bloody doctor, I need Valentina!"

"Yes, sir. Understood, sir." The agent backed out of the room and shut the door, then turned to the secretary. "Call Dr. Willoughby. I think the President is having an episode."

The doctor arrived and the agent hurried him into the Oval Office. Jackson was pacing the room, still yelling for Valentina. Half of the rebuilt Resolute desk had been wiped clear and the papers, pens, folders and decorations were scattered across the floor.

"Mr. President, sir. Dr. Willoughby is here to see you," the agent said. Willoughby set his bag down and proceeded to fill a hypodermic with a sedative while the agent tried to get Jackson to sit down.

"No, you don't understand! I just spoke to her the other day. I promised her I'd try and do the right thing. I promised..." JJ's voice trailed off as the doctor stepped up behind him and stuck him in the thigh with the hypodermic.

"Catch him," Willoughby told the agent as the sedative took effect and the President slumped over. The agent gently lay him on one of the two sofas in the room, lifting his feet and pulling off his shoes before settling them up on the sofa so JJ was lying more comfortably. "Do you have any idea what upset him?" Willoughby asked the agent.

"Sir, he's been increasingly erratic over the past month. Since the E street bombing, it's been worse. Some of his friends and associates were killed that day."

"I see."

"The National Security director was here about an hour ago, giving him a briefing. Maybe that pushed him over the edge?"

"It's possible. But why would he be calling for his sister? Hasn't she been dead for over twenty-five years or so?" Willoughby asked. "She has," the agent replied, then hesitated. "If I may add, sir. About a week ago, his daughter, her fiancé, the Vice President and his partner were here, and I was on duty at the inside door."

Willoughby nodded as he crouched to take the President's vitals.

"He started talking to his sister then, staring at something that I couldn't see, holding what appeared to be a full conversation with her."

Willoughby arched a brow and looked up at the agent. "What did the others do?"

"They sat there, not saying a thing, while he held this conversation."

"So, they witnessed his bizarre behavior. That helps." Willoughby stood, disposed of the syringe and closed his bag. "I'll have him transported to the hospital. He needs to be kept under sedation and monitored. We'll gradually decrease the sedation and see if he is still distraught. I'll make sure the psychologists are brought in to talk to him. Call Matthews. He's going to have to take over for a couple of weeks."

"I'll set the protocols in motion, Dr. Willoughby," the agent replied as he stepped out of the room.

The doctor sighed as he looked down at the unconscious man. "Well, you fucked it good this time, Jackson. I can't cover this up."

Emlen had been working on her laptop, the TV on in the background, when her phone rang. "Em here," she answered.

"Em, it's Edmund. Jackson has just been admitted to Walter Reed on a seventy-two hour psych hold. They had to sedate him in the Oval because he was screaming for Valentina."

"Oh, holy shit," Em said.

"Yeah. They've invoked the 25th and I'm acting President right now."

"Are you okay?"

"I'm good. I'm going to see what I can do to clear up some of the backlog and get things moving again. He's not been working well the last week or so. I also need to call Thomas and Connor. PLEA needs to step in and clean up what's left of the Order. I have a stack of messages and emails that he's ignored about properties all over the world that have been ransacked and raided by the Order's soldiers with no one left to run the thing."

"Well, at least he isn't blaming the Garda for that bombing."

"No, I think he knows that's so far from what the Garda would have done, and the exact opposite of what PLEA would do," Edmund said.

"If you need us for anything, Edmund, just ask, okay?"

"I will, Em. Patrick's here and I'll make those calls. Tell the planners to come to you or Patrick for any wedding questions. I have an overflowing plate here."

"I'll take care of it, Edmund. Go be awesome."

"Thanks Em," Edmund said and disconnected the call.

Emlen texted Cullen instead of shouting through the house. "Edmund is acting President. JJ is at Walter Reed on psych hold."

A few minutes later, Cullen showed up with a smoothie and a kiss before he settled into the chair beside her. "Here, I brought you strawberry banana goodness."

"I love you," Emlen said.

"I know. So, what happened with JJ?"

"Apparently, he was trashing the Oval and screaming for Valentina. Willoughby sedated him and had him transported to Walter Reed for a psych eval. They invoked the 25th and Edmund is acting President. He's going to call Thomas and Connor and get PLEA to take care of the mess the bombing of the Order left behind. It seems a bunch of the Order's soldiers ransacked the bases and disappeared."

"Great. Just what we needed. A bunch of armed lunatics with no leadership."

Emlen sighed. "I know, it's nuts. Oh, I only have about thirty more files to go through and I'll be done. So far, I've found twenty-three potentials. There's something weird, though."

"What's that?"

"Five of these guys were in Spain from about two months ago until about two weeks ago, just around the time of the bombing. Now they're in Ireland. At least, that's what their financials are telling me."

"Ireland? Where in Ireland?" Cullen asked.

"Dublin," Emlen replied.

Chapter Nine

Jackson was back behind his desk in the Oval and Edmund was sitting in a meeting with Emlen, Patrick, and Cullen at Mayfield. Three weeks had passed since JJ had to be sedated and he was now being monitored by Willoughby on a daily basis. The press had been told that the President had to be hospitalized for kidney stones and that he was now well enough to work half days. In reality, he was on antidepressants and mood stabilizers, making the daily monitoring a critical necessity since he often refused to take his medication.

The two couples were finalizing the last few decisions for the weddings with their planners and the White House coordinator. Emlen was so done with the questions. A long sigh and she looked up at Margaret, the White House coordinator.

"Okay, let me make sure I have this right. We've made decisions about the cake, flowers, colors, invitations, and about sixteen hundred other things. I have my dress and shoes, the people standing up with me and their outfits all arranged. Cullen has his tux and his guys all set. We even have rings – well, Cullen's taking care of that. Now I have to decide on bridal party gifts? Is that the absolute last thing I have to deal with?"

"Yes, that should be it," Margaret replied.

"Good, because I swear, I'm about ready to just elope."

Margaret, her assistant Amy, and Kitty, the wedding planner, all looked like they were going to faint.

"Oh, no, you can't do that," Margaret replied. "The American people are eager to see the nuptials and the event already has broadcast times and..."

Cullen slid an arm around Emlen. "What my fiancée is saying is that if you're all supposed to be handling the details, then handle the details. We just want to get married."

Patrick chuckled. "That's pretty much where we are with all of this. At least we don't have to change tuxes, just where we're standing from one wedding to the next."

"Also, when the President walks you down the aisle," Kitty said.

"I'm sorry, when who does what?" Emlen asked.

Kitty blinked at her. "When the President, your father, walks you down the aisle, the cameras will follow front and back."

"The President is not walking me down the aisle. James O'Brien is."

"But..." Kitty started to argue.

Emlen got to her feet. "My father was not in my life until a few short months ago. He has not earned the right to walk me anywhere. He can sit in the front row and watch. He's not participating." With that, Emlen walked out of the room.

Everyone was silent for a moment and then Cullen smiled. "I guess we'll see you in a few days. Do have a safe trip back to DC." Then he followed Em from the room.

He found her in the conservatory, hands curled into fists as she paced.

"Emmy," Cullen said as he stepped into the room.

She turned and hurried over to him to wrap her arms around his waist. "I really wish we just eloped," she mumbled into his chest.

"No, love, you don't. You know how proud Da is going to be, walking you down the aisle? How thrilled Camille will be, seeing her little girl get married? How much Ma is going to be fussing over us both? All they've wanted is to see us happy and make them lots of grandbabies."

Emlen snorted laughter into his shirt. "Yeah, Ma texts or calls me every day to see how I'm doing. And yes, I want to wear my granny's gown and make my promises to you in front of our family and friends. I just didn't want the bloody three ring circus."

Cullen ran his hands up and down her back as he soothed her. "Just think, someday we'll be able to tell our kids and grandkids that we got married in the White House Rose Garden."

Em tipped her head back and looked up at him. "I love you, Cullen Murphy O'Brien and I can't wait until I'm Emlen O'Brien at last."

He leaned down and kissed her, then pulled her close and rested his chin on her head. "I know it's a lot right now, Em. Once the weddings are over, I can walk down the street with you and not worry about who might see us. I won't worry about whether JJ will come after us for loving each other. It will make things better for us both."

"You're right, it will take a lot of pressure off us. I just want to get back to Boston and enjoy getting the house ready for our baby."

"Now that sounds like a plan," Cullen said and kissed her again. "Let's finish up our work for today so we can have a movie night in our room."

"Deal," Em said and gave him a smile. "But I'm picking the movie this time."

"I thought you liked comedies?"

"I don't like stupid comedies. Besides, I'm in the mood for something with lots of explosions."

Cullen laughed as they walked out of the room.

JJ sat at the Resolute desk, a stack of business cards in front of him. He had been building a card house and had two levels done already when his Chief of Staff entered. "What do you want, Thompson?"

The man hesitated when he saw what the President was doing, then cleared his throat. "Mr. President, you have a meeting with the Joint Chiefs in fifteen minutes and we still need to go over your talking points for the State of the Union address tomorrow."

"I don't want to talk to them. All they talk about is armies and war, combat strategies. It's boring."

"Uh, sir, you have to talk to them."

"No, I don't," JJ said.

"Yes, sir, you do. And you must do the State of the Union address. The Congress and the whole country is expecting it."

JJ slammed his hand on the desk and the card tower tumbled across the polished surface and onto the floor. "I do not have to do it! I'm the President! I make all the rules." He whined as he looked down. "Now look at what you made me do. This is all your fault, Thompson. Leave. You're fired."

Thompson sighed. "Again, sir? Fine. I'll be back in an hour."

JJ mumbled to himself as he picked up the business cards and sat down as he started to build the tower once more.

Thompson shook his head and left the room.

Dr. Willoughby had been called in to check the President's medication levels and some adjustments were made. The man that walked into the chamber to give the State of the Union address barely resembled the man who had recently been building a card house on his desk. Introductions were made and he took his place at the podium, the teleprompter flashing in front of him.

"My fellow Americans," he began, then read through the first few minutes of the prepared speech. He paused and leaned one arm on the podium as he looked at the camera and not at the prompter. "You know what? We're the greatest country in the world. We have the best land, the best people, and it's all because of people like me." He leaned back then, hands curled against the sides of the podium. "People with magic have made this country great."

Gasps echoed through the chamber.

"Yes, magic. Controlling your impulses, protecting you against those who would have corrupted our great country. Magic and my ability to wield it is just one example. There are thousands of us who have gifts and powers beyond your understanding. Be grateful! If not for me..."

Edmund finally made his way up to the podium with Dr. Willoughby and they got JJ to turn to speak to them. Secret Service got the live feed shut down and commercials were run.

"Mr. President," Edmund said. "You can't be talking about this. It's not safe."

"I'm the President. I can talk about whatever I want," JJ argued.

"No, sir, you cannot. We don't discuss magic with mundanes, you know this," Edmund whispered in his ear.

"I'm the greatest president this country has ever seen and they all deserve to know why," JJ roared, the mics and those nearby hearing every bit of that sentence.

Willoughby sighed and with a nod from Edmund, he jabbed JJ once more. Agents lifted JJ over to a stretcher and he was taken from the chamber. Edmund leaned over to whisper to the Speaker of the House who nodded back at him as he turned and stepped up to the podium. A nod to the cameras and he took a deep breath.

"The recent illness the President suffered caused him to be put on medication that has, it appears, caused a bad reaction. He is being flown to Walter Reed Hospital where his personal physician and specialists will evaluate him. Keep our President in your prayers. Good night." Edmund turned and stepped down to polite applause, exiting the room with Patrick at his side.

They stepped into a smaller room where the Speaker of the House joined them. "Well, Matthews, it looks like you're acting President once more. This time, it just might stick. We can't have a raving lunatic in the White House."

"Yes, Madame Speaker. I had hoped Willoughby had balanced his medication by now. Perhaps the mental illness his father suffered is a family trait?" Edmund replied.

"It's starting to look that way," the Speaker said. "Well, I'll get my update in the morning. Go get some sleep. You've got a seat to fill tomorrow." She paused and glanced back at him. "Congratulations on your upcoming wedding. That's next week, correct?"

"Yes, Madame Speaker. Six days from today," Edmund said.

"I'm looking forward to it. Goodnight, gentlemen."

The room slowly emptied and Patrick turned to Edmund. "See? I told you. First Partner."

They both chuckled wearily before following their agents out to the car to take them back to the Observatory. It was going to be a very long week.

The news the next morning was all about Jackson and his raving about magic. The magical community was furious and doing its best to not overreact, but word had spread that if Jackson was put back as President, they'd have to permanently remove him. Emlen and Cullen shared breakfast in silence as they watched the various reports. As they finished, Emlen picked up the dishes and brought the coffee pot back to refresh their cups.

"So, what are you thinking?" Cullen finally asked her. "You've been awful quiet."

Emlen shrugged. "I'm not sure. I mean, yeah, I feel bad because I wonder if I'm not partly responsible for him going crazy. He didn't really go wholly over the edge until Tina talked to him. I guess her being killed when he was a kid really messed him up more than anyone thought."

"It seems that way, yeah. But he also just lost his father and had a ton of unresolved issues with the man, then lost his right hand guy, Dunleavy. Never mind the whole Order leadership getting blown up in one night. Well, all but JJ and that one old guy in London who had a heart attack and died after watching the whole thing on camera," Cullen said. "You cannot take the blame for this, Em. I love that you're kind hearted enough to actually feel sorry for the asshole, but it's not all on you." Cullen leaned over and gave her a soft kiss. "Let it go, love. He's doing for us what we needed to get done. He's not going to be able to stay President and he'll probably end up locked up like his father. Out of power and out of our way." He paused and looked at his phone. "Don't you have training with Ryan and Kian in ten minutes? Better get moving."

Em groaned and finished her coffee. "Yeah, but at least they've promised me something different this time. Not sure what, but as long as it's not more Krav Maga I'll be happy."

A few minutes later, Em stood outside in the field behind the house with Ryan and Kian. They'd set up metal posts with three discs on each post to resemble head, chest, and legs. There were eight of them placed at various angles and distances. Ryan jogged up to where she stood with Kian, a huge grin on his face. "Ready for some fun?" Em still looked confused. "What am I doing, jousting? I don't get it." Kian laughed.

"Fireball target practice. We figured you were getting sick of shooting at a brick wall and this way you can practice a bit more realistically."

"Oh, now that's a good idea," Emlen said. "Okay, you guys stay behind me. I don't know how good my aim is going to be at first." They moved to stand behind her and to each side as Em closed her eyes and took a couple of slow breaths. Centered and focused, she felt the tingling energy building in her core, then as she focused on the closest target, her hand came up, palm out, and a pulse of energy flew at the disks. The center disk on the closest target changed from silver to black.

"Direct hit!" Kian called out.

"I had Stefan charm them so that a glancing blow turns it red, a direct hit, black." Ryan said.

"Now that is awesome," Em said and took a few more shots. "The head shots are harder, I keep getting red on those. But now I can finesse my aim with practice." She turned and hugged Ryan first, then Kian. "You guys are the best."

"Yeah, we know," Ryan said as he gave Kian a high-five. "So, while we're gone, you keep practicing. The colors will reset after about thirty minutes."

"What do you mean, while you're gone?"

"Kian and I are headed to Dublin the day after the wedding to check on the financial trail from the E Street bombing. Connor and Thomas asked us to take a look since I used to work in financial terrorism and Kian's a signals guy."

"Well, you guys stay safe. And Ryan, if you want to bring your ex to the wedding, you can. I know you're still friends," Emlen said.

"Gina would love to come. She's doing well in Boston, but a long weekend in DC would be fun for us both. I'll see what she says," Ryan replied.

"What about you, Kian?" Em asked. "You bringing anyone?"

"Hell no," Kian laughed. "Weddings are the best place to pick up girls."

"Okay, go on, you two. I'm going to practice a little more before I go back into the office. Thanks, guys. I mean it. Between the two of you, I've grown as a magician and a person," Em told them. They waved her off with smiles as they headed back in and Em turned to the targets. This was going to be fun.

Chapter Ten

The day of the wedding dawned clear and bright. A rain shower the night before left everything with that fresh-washed feeling. Cooler temperatures but not cold had Emlen happy she wouldn't be chilled in her gown. The antique lace and satin had been cleaned, mended, and fit her like a glove. High neck, long sleeves that ended in points over her hands, a fitted bodice and tucked waist that spilled into a narrow bell-shaped skirt with a short train. The original veil fell to her waist, held into her thick auburn hair with a jeweled clip. Cream satin kitten heels, the antique amethyst set from the Emmerson side that brought out the clear violet hue of her eyes and a lace-edged handkerchief that had been her grandmother Simone's, completed the picture. She'd had her hair put up in a modernized Gibson girl style with ringlet tendrils and jeweled pins.

As she stood in front of the full-length mirror, the ghosts of her mother, Camille and her grandmother, Simone, stood with her. Eileen O'Brien and Susan fussed about the room before Susan handed her the bouquet of peach and cream roses with tiny fronds of wheat and trails of ivy tangling with peach and cream silk ribbon.

"You look incredible," Simone said, eyes bright as she took in the vision of her granddaughter. "May you find every happiness, dear girl."

"Thank you, Grandma Simone," Emlen replied. Eileen and Susan kissed her cheek and left her to find their seats with a few last words of love and encouragement. Simone faded away and left Emlen alone with her mother.

Camille gently hugged Emlen and kissed her cheek. "My beautiful daughter. You've made me so proud in so many ways, but seeing you here today, ready to promise yourself to the love of your life? That makes my heart so full. You've come so far, Em. From that hurt, bitter girl who did whatever she wanted, regardless of the consequences, to a woman who fights for those she loves and for what is right. I love you so much, Emlen. I'll be watching this whole day and soaking up all of the love and beauty. Shine, my girl. Let them see your incredible light."

Emlen made sure to breathe through the threatened tears. "Mom, you're gonna make me cry and ruin my makeup." They both laughed and Em leaned over to kiss Camille's cheek. "I love you, Mom. I am really glad you're here with me."

"Always, my girl. Until we both decide it's time for me to move on, I'll always be with you."

The sound of trumpets drifted through the open French doors and James O'Brien knocked before he poked his head around. "Ready, my girl?"

"Ready, Da," Em replied and walked towards him. A black tux with white vest and tie and a peach rose boutonniere for the men looked sharp on James. Em slid her hand over his arm and whispered, "Don't let me trip, Da. I don't need that flashed across the globe."

James chuckled low and patted her hand. "I'd never let you down, my girl. My daughter at last."

Em reached up and kissed his cheek as they waited for the music to change. A white aisle runner stretched from the building to the arch where Mari and Connor, acting as matron of honor and best man, stood beside clergy from the National Cathedral. Cullen stood near the center, dressed like his father and brother, with a white rose in his lapel.

Emlen's eyes locked with Cullen's and neither seemed to see anyone else as she slowly approached. James kissed Emlen's cheek, then stepped back to stand in the front row next to Eileen before everyone sat. Emlen handed her bouquet to Mari and turned to take Cullen's hands in hers.

He met her gaze and whispered, "You look incredible."

The bishop welcomed family and friends before she announced that the couple had written their own vows. Emlen and Cullen stared into each other's eyes and spoke together. "Above us are the moons and stars, below us are the stones, as time does pass, I will remember. Like a stone should our love be firm. Like a star should our love be constant. Let the powers of the mind and of the intellect guide us. Let the strength of our wills bind us together. Let the power of love and desire make us happy, and the strength of our dedication make us inseparable. Be close, but not too close. Possess one another yet be understanding. Have patience with one another, for storms will come, but they will pass quickly. Be free in giving affection and warmth, for love endures all things."

They were each then asked if they took the other and each said, "I do."

Connor handed them the rings and in less than fifteen minutes, they were pronounced husband and wife. A kiss and they made their way back down the aisle to the applause and good wishes of the four hundred people filling the seats around them. They stopped under the roof overhang and kissed again before walking up the side aisle and taking their seats in the front row.

Thomas moved up to stand where Connor had been and Patrick's brother, Michael, took Mari's place. Music swelled and everyone rose as first Patrick, walking with his parents and then Edmund, walking with his sister Elaine, made their way up to the bishop.

The two stood together and recited a modified version of the traditional vows, naming each other husband and partners in love and life before they exchanged rings and a kiss. They held hands as they made their way back up the aisle to cheers and applause.

Emlen and Cullen met them at the back where the attendants and families gathered for the photo shoot while the guests went inside to the reception. They'd laughed a lot during the photo shoot and made their grand entrances into the reception with bright smiles and joyous hearts. The White House chefs had outdone themselves with two cakes and an exquisite menu. Everything seemed perfect, except for the few muttered comments about President Jackson missing his daughter's wedding. After about the fifth carefully whispered pity comment, Emlen got to her feet and tapped her glass with a spoon until the room was mostly silent.

"Thank you all for coming to share this wonderful day with us. However, as you all know, President Jackson has been ill. Yes, his absence is felt, but as you also know, we didn't know each other until about a year ago. The man who walked me down the aisle is not only the father of my heart, but now my father by marriage. I could not be more satisfied with how the day has gone and wish President Jackson all the healing he deserves." As she took her seat once more, a light smattering of applause rang out and people soon found other things to discuss.

"Nicely phrased," Mira commented from beside her. "May the Powers that Be hear your prayer."

They both started to laugh softly and Mira shook her head. "We didn't want to do the official change over until after the wedding, but Edmund is going to be sworn in as President. Jackson is too far gone to serve any longer. I got the word last night that he is entering long-term psychiatric care."

"I hate to say it, but I'm glad. We needed him out and now he's out. But what if he influences someone with his telepathy to let him go?"

"PLEA has a neuro-blocker that works on telepaths. He's getting regular doses so he can't use his gift."

Emlen let out a breath and relaxed. "Good. Best news I've heard in a while."

James approached the table and held out his hand to Emlen. "Ready for the father – daughter dance, little one?"

Emlen smiled and rose, hand placed in his. They danced to "Butterfly Kisses" and by the time they were done, there were very few dry eyes in the room.

Em danced with Cullen, Connor, Edmund, Patrick, Ryan, Kian, and every other member of the team based at Mayfield. The rest of the evening was a joyful celebration of life and love.

The next morning the front hall of Mayfield was filled with luggage as Emlen, Cullen, Kian and Ryan prepared to fly to Boston and meet up with Connor. From there, the five of them would head to Dublin. Scatha was staying behind at Mayfield because caging the raven for transport was too risky. Tina was keeping an eye on JJ and any visitors he might have before joining them later. Edmund and Patrick were spending the weekend at the beach before returning to DC for his swearing in as President, while Susan and Angelica were leaving later in the day to settle in for the winter in Muckle Cove. A few of the PLEA staff would still be in residence, but the house was emptying fast.

Joel paced while Cullen gave some last minute directions to the staff staying behind.

Emlen sighed, "Joel, stop. You're making me queasy with all your circling."

"Sorry, Emmy, but I have a really bad feeling about this trip. You should be staying here, where it's safe."

"Right, where I was shot at and Susan was almost killed. Real safe."

"You know what I mean," Joel said. "Safer than in a city in a foreign country."

"You're worrying over nothing. We need to be in Dublin for work and then we're going to Galway for a honeymoon. Just go fade out and wait for the overseas flight to pop back, will ya?"

Cullen wrapped an arm around Em. "What's wrong?"

"Joel's all wound up about the trip. Says he has a bad feeling about it. I think he's just not happy about the flight," Em replied.

"Well, he always hated flying, so you may be right. We'll just be extra cautious in case he's picking up on something," Cullen said.

A horn sounded from the front of the house and everyone moved out. Cases and bags were loaded, hugs were given and soon they were on the flight to Boston. Once they landed, everything was transferred to PLEA's private jet and they settled in for the longer flight. Connor looked exhausted as he'd had to fly back to Boston after the wedding last night to deal with a minor crisis and then get everything loaded for the trip today. Once they were in the air, Connor slipped on his headset and went to sleep. Kian and Ryan were soon dozing as well and Emlen had stretched out the seat so she could curl up against Cullen's side.

Em stared at the rings on her hand as she tapped her fingers on Cullen's chest. "I think that looks pretty cool," she said.

Cullen, who had been reading on his tablet, looked up. "Huh?"

"My rings. I think they look cool. I never imagined my life like this, but I'm liking it – and the symbolism is pretty nice." Custom knotwork bands set with tiny amethysts wrapped both of their fingers. It went beautifully with the band of channel set stones he'd given her as an engagement ring. On her right hand, she wore the heirloom ring Edmund had given her for their fake engagement. When she'd tried to give it back, he told her to keep it as it was imbued with protection spells and he wanted her and the babe protected.

"It's funny. I lost the amber pendant my Mom gave me when I released my magic, but I've gained so much more. I used to consider that my best piece of jewelry. Now I have these rings that symbolize love, promises, and protection. I count myself blessed."

Cullen leaned over and kissed her forehead. "I'm the blessed one."

Emlen slept the rest of the flight. She woke when the plane landed, taking the warm towel and wiping her face and hands to wake herself more fully. Connor and Kian were chatting as they gathered a few things and Cullen had been playing cards with Ryan.

Laughter and camaraderie filled the cabin as they greeted the Customs agent when she stepped onto the plane and signed the paperwork to welcome them to Ireland. A hired car drove them to the outskirts of Dublin where they would be staying. Once, the manor had belonged to the Garda, now it belonged to the O'Briens and was used for PLEA agents that needed to spend time in the city.

Gray stone rose three stories with a rounded tower at one corner. A slate-shingled roof, white trim on the windows, and a bright red door beckoned to them. A gated drive, tall stone walls, and beautiful landscaping gave the place the feel of a castle.

"It's gorgeous," Emlen said as she stood in the curved gravel drive and looked around.

"I'd seen photos of when Joel stayed here once and always wanted to come," Cullen replied. "It has eight bedrooms, nine bathrooms, a garden out back, and an awesome patio and porch with a huge stone heated spa pool."

Em rolled her shoulders and gave Cullen a wink. "We're checking out the spa pool sooner rather than later."

Connor passed them, carrying a couple of bags. "Not until after the meeting in fifteen minutes. Pick out your room, take a minute to freshen up and we'll be in the dining room. It's to the left of the front door. There are three rooms open on the second floor and two on the third. I recommend you take the big one in the back right corner on the second. Has a nice bath, a small balcony and an awesome view. My usual room is the same but on the left back corner."

Cullen saluted Connor's back and Emlen laughed.

"Don't be a dick, bro," Connor said, not having turned to look. "There will be food for the meeting..." he trailed off, letting the tease linger as Em and Cullen shouldered bags and headed in.

The room was decorated in shades of green with white accents and Emlen loved it. All of the furniture they'd seen in the house looked antique and solid, yet not out of character for the rooms. A carved head and foot board in dark wood, a matching dresser that looked almost Victorian, had been paired with a comfortable love seat and delicate side tables. The bathroom was more American style than European, with a soaking tub and a separate glass-walled shower. A window was open next to the tub and in the bedroom, drapes were pulled back to show the arched French doors that led out onto a small stone balcony. A wrought iron bistro set had been perfectly placed for morning coffee and the view of the fields, ending in the glint of coastal waters.

"Morning coffee out here is going to be perfect," Emlen said as she brushed out her hair then tugged it into a high ponytail. "I hope they've got more than snacks. We're hungry."

Cullen chuckled, "I love when you talk about the two of you together. Let's go feed you both." They stepped out into a hall that ran in a long rectangle around the staircase with the steps up to the third floor at the front of the house and the opening to go down at the back. The upper banister was polished and straight while the lower gleamed in a sinuous curve as the steps widened near the bottom.

Emlen leaned over to whisper to Cull, "I wish I wasn't pregnant. I'd slide down this banister."

Cullen paused, gave her a wink, and threw his leg over the banister, sliding down backwards with his hands slowing the pace in front of him.

"Not fair," Emlen called out, laughing as she hurried down to catch up at the bottom. They laughed all the way to the dining room where they settled into two chairs near Connor's. Kian and Ryan hadn't come back down yet but there were two new faces across the table.

Connor set down his glass and made the introductions. "Aoife, Sean, this is my brother Cullen and his wife, Emlen. Aoife is the communications expert for PLEA here in Ireland and Sean is one of the best tactical snipers I've ever met."

"Nice to meet you," Emlen said as Cullen stood and shook their hands.

"Are you President Jackson's daughter?" Aoife asked.

"Yeah, sort of. I mean, he's my bio-dad but he didn't raise me. And we have a new President as of tomorrow. President Edmund Matthews."

"Weren't you engaged to him?" Aoife continued.

"It was something Jackson wanted but Edmund is more like an uncle or brother than a partner. Besides, he's married to

Patrick. He never liked girls. We just did it to keep Jackson from killing us."

Aoife blinked a few times at that and went quiet as a young woman came in and started placing dishes on the table. Potatoes, a roast, carrots, and fresh rolls were laid out.

"It looks delicious, Mary. Thank you," Connor said.

"Simple fare it may be, but I think you'll enjoy it. The butter is fresh from Murphy's farm up the road," Mary said.

"Thank you, Mary," Emlen said.

Mary smiled as she left the room, coming back with a pitcher of iced tea and one of water. Everyone dished up food as they passed bowls and plates around the table. Kian and Ryan arrived just as people started to eat and got their food before making introductions.

"Edmund and Patrick will be in Dublin in two days. We'll be backing up their Secret Service contingent while they're in town," Connor said.

"Aoife will manage the communications and Emlen will assist wherever needed."

"Sounds good," Cullen replied. "Are there more PLEA agents in town?"

"Four more will be arriving and staying at the hotel with the President and his partner." Sean paused and took a sip of his drink. "Is there any particular reason why so many PLEA agents are on call for the President?"

"Yes," Cullen replied. "He's a magic user, as is his partner. In fact, Edmund is the head of our coven. He feels safer having a few of his own kind around."

"Well, that makes a lot more sense," Aoife replied. Joel showed up on the other side of the table between Aoife and Sean.

"Emlen, there are four men in black suits that pulled up outside the gate, using binoculars to try and see the house."

Em turned to Connor. "Joel says there are four men in black suits parked outside the gate using binoculars."

Kian and Ryan got to their feet. "We'll check it out," Ryan said as they headed out the door. Connor nodded and reached under the table to press a button. Metal shutters lowered over the windows throughout the house. "Better to be safe than sorry," he said as he rose to his feet.

Cullen got up to follow, as did Sean. "Em, stay inside please. You were their target last time, let's not give them what they want," Connor said before he headed out into the foyer.

A sigh and Em nodded as she picked at her food. Aoife watched the whole thing, eyes wide.

"What the hell is going on?" Aoife asked.

"The rogue group you've been hunting? They tried to take me out in Maryland and nearly killed an older woman I consider family. I can't do my usual and ignore the warnings and go help because I'm pregnant."

"Well, that'd put a crimp in anyone's day, eh?" Aoife said as she picked up her fork.

Em snorted laughter. "That's one way of putting it." "You should come meet my Grandmother. She could tell you what you're having," Aoife offered. "She lives about a mile down the road."

Emlen thought about it for a moment, then grinned. "Yeah, that might be interesting. Is she a magic user?"

"She calls herself a Cailleach. It's what the old ones call a witch or a goddess. I've seen her heal the worst injuries and light a fire in her hearth or a candle without a match."

"Now that's cool. I look forward to meeting her and perhaps learning from her," Em said. She pushed to her feet and headed into the foyer. "I can't stand not knowing what's going on."

"Just don't open the door. There's a peep hole in each shutter and in the door. The walls are over a foot thick of stone and the shutters are bullet proof," Aoife said.

Em got to the door just as it opened, the men headed back inside. "What happened? Who were they?"

Cullen gave her a hug and turned to Kian and Ryan.

Ryan spoke. "They said they were agents of someone named Peter Wolfe and that we had a week to remove ourselves from Ireland or suffer the consequences."

Everyone looked confused. Connor looked at each one. "Do any of you have any clue who this Peter Wolfe might be?"

A lot of head shakes and no answers.

"Okay, Aoife and Cullen, you hit the command center and see if you can dig up anything on this Wolfe. Em? I need you to pull up those files I had you scanning. Two of those four I'm sure were ex-Garda. Ryan, Kian, and Sean, you patrol and check the perimeter and the house defenses. I'm going to see if Thomas has any idea what we're dealing with."

Ryan stepped up to Connor, "I think we just were introduced to the rogues and got their leader's name."

Connor nodded. "I think you're right."

Chapter Eleven

Peter Wolfe sat as still as his pain-wracked body would allow while the doctor ran his tests and scans. He had waited months for this appointment with the best specialist in the world. He didn't really have any hope that there would be something that could help, but he had the means and resources, so he had to try. Hope faded to ash when he saw the doctor's face a few hours later.

"I'm sorry, Mr. Wolfe. The work that has been done previously was excellent. There is nothing more I can do to improve your situation."

Peter sighed. "As I expected, doctor. I appreciate your time and efforts." A nod of his head and his aide began to push his chair from the room.

The doctor cleared his throat and looked at Wolfe. "One more thing, Mr. Wolfe. The damage has caused a slow, systemic failure of several of your organs. I regret to inform you that you may only have a few months of life remaining."

Wolfe gave the doctor a faint smile. "I know that, doctor. I had just hoped to find a way to make these last months less difficult. I do appreciate your time. Good day."

They left the room and the doctor shook his head. He'd had a lot of strange patients, but that one was a study for the medical journals. There was, in his estimation, no good reason the man should still be breathing. It made no sense. He sat down and started going over all of the lab results and notes once more. There had to be some reason why the man was still on this side of the turf.

Settled before his monitors, Peter looked out at the stormy Irish weather. A fire burned on the hearth on the other side of the room, far from his precious equipment. It made him feel warmer just to see it, even if his body didn't truly register temperature properly any longer. A shaking finger pushed the lever and the monitors showed the cameras panning the regions they were placed within, exposing the location of the G20 summit to his gaze. Satisfied that he had all of the venue points covered, he flipped the lever again and brought up another building. This one was two stories, stone, and hosted the PLEA offices in Dublin. It used to be a Garda base and he had known the layout as well as his own home.

"Don't worry, my Valentina. I will finish my task before I join you. We're close now," he whispered as he checked each camera.

The cameras he used now were different than those he used in DC for the Order's meeting. One of his men had an exceptional gift of melding magic and technology. These in the PLEA office were special and he couldn't wait to see how well they performed.

The lobby was full of out of town PLEA agents who had gathered for the G20 as support for the United States President's visit and the attendance of the upper echelon of PLEA. Peter knew he should wait, but he couldn't hold back. He had to see how well these worked before the big day.

Watching the cameras, he saw a large group move into one of the conference rooms and switched the video to that room. As nearly thirty members sat down around the conference table and stood along the walls, he pushed the button. And laughed.

Ryan pulled up to the stone building and shut off the car. He glanced over at Kian and nudged him. "Wake up, man. We're here."

Kian groaned, rubbed his face and sat up, reaching for the cup in the holder at his side. The coffee was still warm enough to be palatable, so he downed it. "I'll be glad when this summit is over. I need sleep that isn't interrupted by some crisis or another. Although, the power going out in the building for ten whole minutes isn't a crisis in my estimation."

"It could have been an attack or an attempt at infiltration," Ryan said.

"Yeah, yeah. But it was a popped fuse. Too many assholes plugging in their chargers," Kian replied.

They climbed out of the car and grabbed their bags, taking in the busy street as they locked the car and hefted their gear.

"Are you sure that's all it was?" Ryan asked.

"Well, we checked everything else. Even the computer security logs. Let's face it, with the increase in personnel for the G20, it's been a nightmare tracking everything anyway.

The usual contingent here is, what, maybe fifty people tops? We've got over two hundred in and around Dublin now."

"And easily half that in the building today with the planning and tactics meetings we're doing. Maybe before the lunch break we can do a walk through with one of the regulars and see if they notice anything," Ryan said.

Kian sighed, "Yeah, as long as I don't miss lunch too. I'm already hungry. You go ahead into the meeting, I'm going to grab something from the kiosk in the lobby."

"Get me a coffee, please," Ryan said as he turned off down the hallway.

"You got it," Kian replied and got in line. He watched the two customers in front of him get their orders, then stepped up. "Hi Evan. I'd like two large coffees, black and one of those egg and cheese sandwich things."

Evan handed him his coffee and left the second on a tray while he started the sandwich. "How are ya today, Kian? Did you see the game last night?"

Kian opened his mouth to answer and his ears popped. Eyes wide, he stared at Evan as something shot past Kian and hit him in the chest, blowing him back through the wall of the kiosk and into a pile of rubble. Whirling, Kian ducked as several more of these beams seemed to track from the corners of the room to where people moved. It looked like a video game with lasers. He reached over the stand, grabbed the over-sized stainless counter board and used it like a shield as he started to move. The hallway to the meeting was gone, a pile of rubble in its place. The stairs were collapsed. The only way he could go was towards the front of the building where a wide window once stood. Every few steps, the metal in his hand jerked and bucked as the laser-like things hit it. He spun and blocked as best he could, but it was hard with all of the rubble, debris, and screaming people around him. Five feet to the window and he'd be out. Kian broke into a run and jerked his shield as he blocked the beam headed for his torso. Yet, he missed the one that hit his legs. Suddenly he flew through the air and landed hard against the wall under the window. He tried to get up, but something didn't feel right. Kian glanced down to see what had him pinned, and realized his legs were gone at about his knees. He had the presence of mind to wonder why there was no blood before he passed out, the counter shield lying on top of him. That's where the rescue crews found Kian – alive and unconscious under a stainless steel counter cover, tucked against the base of the window.

He was one of only six to come out of the building alive.

Emlen sat on the balcony outside their bedroom, a cup of tea beside her laptop on the table. The article about her wedding and "Irish honeymoon" was going slow.

Ryan's voice drew her attention to the doorway as he called her name. "Ryan? I thought you were with Kian at the PLEA conferences?" Em rose to her feet when Ryan didn't reply. "Ryan?" She took a few steps closer and frowned. "Ryan, what's wrong? You don't look well." She went to rest a hand on his arm and it passed through. "Oh. Hell, no."

Ryan shook his head and then spoke, "Emlen, can you hear me?"

Em swallowed her tears and nodded. "Yeah, Ryan, I can. What happened?"

"I'm dead, aren't I?" Ryan asked.

"Yeah, hon. You are. I'm so sorry. Do you remember what happened?"

"Sort of. Kian stopped to get coffee at the kiosk and I went in to the conference room. I sat in a chair against the wall because the room was packed. Simon got up to open the meeting and all hell broke loose. Something happened with the security cameras. They started shooting these beams at people and wherever they hit, it blew a hole in them."

"Holy hell," Em whispered. "What kind of weapon does that?"

"I think it was magical. It tracked people as they ran and tried to get out. Blew holes in the walls and caused the structure to fail."

"And Kian?"

"I don't know. I didn't see him. I haven't seen him here, either. I saw a lot of people from the meeting walking into the light, but I needed to tell you what happened," Ryan said.

Emlen reached out to grab his arm and when she felt he was solid, she gave him a hug. "You have been the best teacher anyone could ask for. Thank you for everything." Tears slid down her cheeks as she looked up at him. "Are you going into the light? I can share messages with people if you'd like."

"I think I missed my chance this time, and I don't think I can go without knowing what happened to Kian," Ryan replied.

"Okay, I need to go tell everyone downstairs. You want to come with me?"

Ryan nodded and followed her down. Emlen wiped her cheeks, took a deep breath, and walked into the command center and into chaos. People called out information, answered phones, tapped on keyboards.

Emlen put two fingers in her mouth and let rip a piercing whistle, then reached out and took Ryan's hand. The room stuttered to a standstill as they turned their attention to Em and Ryan. Then Emlen let go of his hand for a moment and took it once more. Gasps and choked out curses rolled through the room as Connor stepped forward and saluted Ryan, fist to chest, head bowed. One by one, the rest of the crew did the same.

Ryan squared his shoulders and returned the salute before he started speaking. "What we thought were security cameras in the rooms had been modified somehow. I think they were tech magicked. They became laser-type weapons that blew holes in anything they hit and tracked people as they tried to escape. Blew holes in walls and destabilized the structure. Kian wasn't in the same room as me, so I don't know what happened to him."

Connor spoke up. "Kian is at the hospital. They found him, and five others, alive. Whatever hit him, one leg is missing from just above the knee, the other just below. No other major injuries. A laser type of weapon fits, because whatever hit him, it cauterized the wounds as it severed the limbs, otherwise he'd be gone too." His voice cracked and he swallowed. "I'm so sorry, brother. What can we do for you, now?"

"Let me help," Ryan said. "I want to do what I can, while I'm here. I want to help figure out who did this and why."

Connor nodded, "As you wish, then. I've sent two men to guard each PLEA member at the hospital. Two of the injured were passing civilians outside the building. Emlen? Are you up for joining Cullen and I at the scene? I need your psychometry skill to see if we can find out anything about those devices."

"Of course, Connor," Emlen replied, glancing over at Cullen.

"As long as you promise to stay glued to my side the whole time," Cullen told her.

"Not a problem," Em said. "Have Edmund and Patrick been updated?"

"About ten minutes before you came down," Connor replied and turned to one of the techs near him. "Let him know what Ryan told us, please."

The tech nodded and moved to his station to contact the President.

Em looked up at Ryan. "I'm going to go get my coat. I'll be right back."

Ryan gave her a faint smile. "Might want to put on some sturdier shoes. There was a lot of debris. Hiking boots if you've got them."

"Good idea." A few minutes later, Emlen, Cullen, Connor and two others waited in the foyer for Michael to bring the SUV around. Ryan had wandered off and said he'd meet them there.

"After we check the place out, I want to go see Kian," Emlen said.

"I do, too," Cullen told her, taking her hand. "He's family and he'll need us. He won't be able to work for a while, if ever again. He's got some hard choices to make, but no matter what, we'll make sure he's taken care of."

"Definitely. Don't want him to worry about anything," Em said.

Connor stepped up and opened the door as the SUV arrived. "Kian won't have to worry about anything, nor will any of our people that were hurt. We will also take care of the families of those that were lost. That's what the Garda used to do, and what PLEA has promised as well."

"Excellent," Emlen said as she slid across the seat, making room for the others to get in. Soon they were all headed to the PLEA offices, tension thick as each wondered what they would find.

It took a while to get through the barricades and rescue vehicles, yet the ride ended over a block from the building. A haze of smoke and dust still swirled in the air as they walked closer, Connor's ID the only thing allowing them this close. As one, they stopped across the road from the building, awed by the sheer amount of destruction.

A fire lieutenant stood beside Connor, explaining what they'd found and where things were now. The lieutenant said it appeared to be some kind of laser weapon that cut through steel and stone as if it were butter. They had put out the fires and shored up the structure so they could continue the search and rescue process. When Connor told him he needed to go inside, the man nearly screamed at him. Connor told him that he would accept all responsibility, insisting national security demanded it and he would not be kept back. Finally, Connor, Cullen, and Emlen were given hard hats, goggles, breathing masks, gloves and reflective vests. The conference room had already been cleared of bodies, so they decided to go there first.

The sight that met them was sobering. Blood had splattered everywhere. On stone, wood, plaster, and glass. Shards of wood from the table mixed with chunks of metal from the chairs and reinforcement beams from the ceiling hung in twisted patterns. Yellow plastic tags with numbers marked where bodies had been recovered.

Emlen looked up as she spotted Ryan standing near the wall. "Is that where you were found?"

He nodded and turned to point up at the corner where what looked like a security camera hung from a wire. "That's one of the weapons."

Emlen pointed to where the camera hung. "I need one of you to get me that. Ryan says it was one of the weapons."

Cullen climbed over the debris and reached up, tugging the camera free of the frayed cord. He came back down and held it out for Emlen. Gingerly, she cupped it in her hands and closed her eyes as she reached for her magic. Images flashed against her closed eyelids and sensations swirled through her body. Emlen's eyes flew open wide and she gasped. "Out...we need to get out..."

Connor reached for the camera as Cullen grabbed Emlen's arm and they started for the exit. Em stumbled and grabbed on to Cullen as they rushed outside. She turned and stared at the building, then at the two brothers. "They're still activated. Get everyone out."

Connor stared at the thing in his hands, then yelped as it began to vibrate. He dropped it on the ground and grabbed a chunk of stone, then smashed the camera until it was fragments while Cullen yelled for the lieutenant to get everyone out.

Screams rang out from the upper level of the building and a figure pressed against a window just as a beam slashed through it and shattered the glass, sending the body tumbling to the ground. Cullen lifted Emlen off her feet and started running back towards their vehicle, Connor not far behind.

Em watched as more windows shattered and the building seemed to slowly fold in upon itself before fully crashing down into a pile of wreckage. Dust billowed into the street and she buried her face in Cullen's shirt, mouth covered as he staggered up to the SUV and practically shoved her inside. He dove in behind her, making sure she was shielded by his body as Connor jumped into the driver's seat. They were headed away from the chaos before Emlen could clear her thoughts.

"Fucking brilliant," Connor hissed as he slowed the SUV down to normal speeds and guided them out of the city. "Someone's been studying their terrorist's handbook. Get the first attack done, then after the place is crawling with first responders, do the second attack."

"Em, are you okay?" Cullen asked as he helped her sit up and get into her seat belt.

"I'm fine, just shaken. I got an image, but I have no idea who the face belongs to. I'll have to sketch it out and see if anyone recognizes him. He was scarred and in a fancy kind of mechanized chair." She shuddered and took a breath. "And he was laughing."

Chapter Twelve

Two days after the attack on the PLEA headquarters, Emlen was checking her makeup in the bathroom mirror. The G20 summit had begun under the most intense security anyone had ever seen.

Camille appeared behind her and smiled at her in the mirror.

"Hi Mom, what's up?"

"Just checking in on you. Wanted to make sure you were okay after the other day. That was too close."

"Yeah, I'm fine. A couple of nightmares, but with Ryan still around and Kian in good spirits, I'm just doing my best to get through the summit and get us home."

"Are we going back to Maryland after?" Camille asked.

"No, Cullen and I want to go back to Boston. It's time to settle down and get ready for the baby." Emlen ran a hand over the slight bulge under her dress and smiled. "I also want to see my doctor in Boston, not deal with a strange doctor in Ireland."

"Just remember to take your vitamins and rest, Emmy," Camille said as she moved to hug her daughter.

"I will, Mom. Gotta go. Love you," Em hugged her back and headed out of the room.

On the stairs, Joel was waiting. "You're okay, yes?" he asked.

"Yes, Joel, I'm fine. The baby's fine. Kian's in good spirits. You've had a chance to talk to Ryan?"

"Yep. Been helping him figure out this ghost business. He always was a quick learner. One of my best students," Joel said.

"Bet you didn't think you'd be teaching still – after death, eh?" Emlen teased him, then kissed his cheek. "I've got to get going. Reception for the summit tonight. Edmund and Patrick asked us to be their special guests, so we've gotta hurry."

"I thought you looked rather nice this evening. Stay safe, little one. I'll be around, watching."

"We'll do our best, Uncle Joel. Don't worry."

The event was held in Clontarf Castle hotel, a beautiful venue about ten minutes outside Dublin city center. Dating to sometime around 1172, the castle's history was evident in the stonework and towers, modernized for comfort and security. Emlen felt like a princess, entering the lobby on Cullen's arm with Connor in front of them, clearing the path. They were stopped repeatedly as Connor greeted various foreign dignitaries and members of the upper ranks of PLEA. They were scanned and screened before entering the function hall, then escorted to Edmund's table where he sat with Patrick, Thomas, and Thomas's partner, Evelyn.

Hugs and handshakes were shared before the three sat and Emlen let out a soft sigh. "I should've worn flat shoes. I'm not going to be able to keep these heels on all night."

Evelyn winced in sympathy. "I heard you were expecting. I lived in ballet flats during both of my pregnancies. What size do you wear?" Emlen told her and Evelyn smiled. "Perfect. For now, slip off your shoes and tuck them under your seat. After dinner, I'll take you up to our rooms and get you something to wear. We're the same size."

"You're a life saver, Evelyn. Thanks," Emlen replied and Cullen chuckled.

"What?" Em asked him.

"I knew we'd have to get maternity clothes eventually. I didn't think about shoes," Cullen said.

Thomas just started to chuckle, then ended up laughing as he warned Cullen, "You have no idea. You'll be buying things for your wife and the baby that you never even knew existed. Welcome to fatherhood, my friend."

Cullen reached for Emlen's hand, squeezing it lightly. "I'll take all of it, and gladly. I can't wait to meet the child we made together."

Emlen had sparkling grape juice while the others had champagne. Once the glasses were filled, Thomas lifted his and looked to Emlen. "To the next Descendant. May the lineage prove true and the blood stay strong."

Everyone tapped their glasses and sipped before dissolving into small pockets of conversation. Emlen, seated beside

Edmund, reached out to rest a hand on his arm. "How are you doing, Edmund? Holding up okay?"

Edmund leaned over to kiss her cheek. "Sweet of you to worry about me, niece, but I'm fine. Patrick and I are doing well and adjusting to the demands of our jobs just fine. No one had time to booby trap the White House residence, so we settled in without any troubles. Have you heard the latest about Jackson?"

"No," Em sighed. "What's he done now?"

"Nothing, that's the thing. No visitors. No demands. He reads several books a week, gets no online time and doesn't watch television. He's reading everything from biographies to romance novels and seems quite content, from all reports." Emlen frowned. "That doesn't sound like him at all. Are we sure it's still JJ they're holding?"

"What? You think he's a doppelganger or something?"

"Who knows? I don't put anything past that man," Emlen replied.

"Wasn't Tina keeping an eye on him?" Patrick asked.

"Yeah, and I have her ring so she can come here if there's anything to report," Emlen said.

"Okay, so if there was something weird going on, she'd have let you know, right?" Edmund asked Em.

"I'm sure she would have. Or she would've told Joel or my mom or someone and they would have let us know, if she was worried about leaving him alone for too long."

"Well, that helps," Edmund said.

"Knowing she's keeping an eye on him." Emlen leaned over, teasing him, "Never let it be said I didn't do my part for the President."

Patrick snorted a soft laugh and shook his head. "Smart ass."

"Anything for family," Emlen laughed and finished her sparkling juice. The meal was excellent and conversation flowed. When Evelyn saw that Em was done with her dessert, she gestured for her to come with her and the two left the room, Emlen carrying her heels.

"How old are your children?" Em asked Evelyn.

"Tasha is twenty-four and Tommy is twenty-two. Tasha works at the UN as an interpreter and Tommy is still at Columbia, majoring in mathematics," Evelyn replied.

They exited the elevator a couple of floors above the function hall and entered the suite. Em took in the elegant furnishings while Evelyn opened a wardrobe and took out a pair of gold ballet flats that would go perfectly with Em's gown. "Here, try these."

Emlen slipped them on and sighed. "Perfect. I meant what I said before, you're truly a life saver." She wiggled her toes and smiled. "I'm going to have to get me a few pairs of these. So, um, Evelyn, may I ask you a kind of personal question?"

"Sure, what's up?" Evelyn replied, taking a seat on the settee beside Em. "Do your kids have magic?"

Evelyn nodded. "Tasha is a telepath and empath. She can read but not plant thoughts or images. Helps her a good deal with her translation work. Tommy is an elemental mage, specializing in water, like me. Why?"

"Because I'm worried about raising a child with magic, who could end up with a whole collection of skills being a Descendant."

"Like with any child, magical or not, boundaries are important. Ethics and morals, right and wrong, the usual things a child needs to learn. There are magic dampening spells I can give you that will help control things if the child exhibits gifts in the preverbal stages. They won't shut the magic off but tone it down to manageable levels. Shutting off a child's magic too early can handicap them later," Evelyn said.

"Mine was hidden and dampened with a charmed jewel when I was small, so while I could still sense ghosts, I couldn't see them or communicate like I can now. None of my other gifts manifested until the jewel was smashed and I got acclimated to my magic. Once I started training and learning, things have been developing," Emlen said. "My mom did that to protect me, though. Hiding me in plain sight and muffling my magic was the best way to keep me safe. She had planned to start teaching me when she was murdered. My grandmother refused to acknowledge magic in any forms, so I didn't know anything or get trained at all until a little over a year ago."

"Wow, that must've been something else," Evelyn said, voice soft. "What..." Just as she started to speak, a wave of something passed through them.

Both gasped as Emlen wrapped her arms around her belly, curled forward instinctively to protect her child. They were both silent, eyes wide as they stare at each other, then Emlen's eyes widened more. "I can hear them. B..both of them."

"Both of whom?" Evelyn asked.

"Both of my babies. I'm carrying twins. A boy and a girl. I can hear their thoughts."

"What the hell was that?" Evelyn said. "I don't know, but we need to get downstairs and find out." Both women rose unsteadily from their seat and made their way to the elevator and back down to the function hall. Raised voices and chaos had spilled out into the hall. Some people cried, others stood around in shock. The two women pushed past people that stumbled and sobbed, headed to the table where their men had been before they left. Secret service agents clustered around Edmund and Patrick while Cullen stood on his chair, gaze on the crowd by the door.

He waved as he spotted them, then climbed down, headed for them through the mass of bodies. Cullen wrapped his arms around Em. "I was worried about you. Something happened," Cullen said.

"We felt it. Two floors up, in Thomas and Evelyn's room. I… " Emlen started to explain, then stopped as the voices around her rose in a crescendo. She slapped her hands over her ears and   the sound didn't stop. Em could see Cullen's lips moving but couldn't hear him through the roar of voices in her head. Soon, the noise grew to be too much and Emlen fainted in Cullen's arms. He lifted her up and carried her out of the hall as Evelyn slipped him her room key and told him to bring her there. She went to get Thomas and the others while Cullen got Em out of the chaos. * * *

Peter watched the monitors, furious that the devices hadn't worked like he had been told they would. "Bring Jonas to me," he ordered, eyes dark with fury. Two of the men left and returned minutes later with Jonas between them. A skinny young man with a mop of blond hair and brown eyes magnified by thick lenses in dark frames.

"Jonas," Peter said, chair turned to greet them. "It seems your devices did not work as planned. What have you got to say for yourself?"

"Did someone bring back one of the devices after it was used?" Jonas asked. Peter turned and nodded to one of the men who brought a plastic bag to Jonas. The young man took the bag and stepped away from his escort to a nearby table. He spilled the contents onto the surface and closed his eyes, took a few slow breaths, and held his hands over the device. It looked like a sensor of some kind; square, black, about three inches across – innocuous and common. A frown settled on Jonas' face and he grunted before he opened his eyes.

"Something tampered with them. A kind of electrical magic charge. It changed them. I don't know exactly what it changed them into, but I can find out."

Peter narrowed his gaze, then turned back to the cameras. "Maybe there's an answer in the video. Go see what you can find." He waved a hand dismissively and Jonas snatched up the device and left the room. Using the control on his chair, Peter inched closer to the monitors and backed up the videos before the event began and started watching. The hotel was supposed to be full of bodies and rubble. Panic and confusion were good, but not sufficient. He had to figure out what had gone wrong.

Chapter Thirteen

Emlen stirred her tea, gaze on the view of the fields and ocean beyond the window. Her other hand rested on the slight swell of her belly as she listened to her babies' thoughts. They were, for the most part, random snippets of emotion and sensation, but Em could tell they liked certain types of music, voices and motion. They enjoyed calming music, got excited when Cullen would be nearby and speaking, and always fell asleep when she was in a car, or when she stood next to the dishwasher as it was running.

The days since the event at the summit reception had been confusing. It seemed that whatever had happened, had awakened Emlen's latent telepathy gift and her fainting spell had been a result of being overwhelmed by too many mental voices. The day after it had happened, Aoife's grandmother, Cathleen, had come by and helped her learn shielding so she could shut out the noise and filter the voices. However, Emlen wasn't the only one affected.

There were still scorch marks on the dining room wall where Cullen had discovered a raised temper brought a flash of lightning to his fingertips and nearly started a fire. Connor had shorted out the electrical system in his car and fried his phone after a particularly heated conversation. Now, both men were outside with Edmund and Patrick, working on their new skills. Edmund's mild telekinetic gift had become much stronger and Patrick's gift with potions was now matched by an elemental skill with water. It seemed that anyone who had a magical bloodline or gift at the event, had either received a power boost or a new skill. Thomas was now a strong telepath as well as getting a boost to his empathy. He could read people up to fifty yards away now, instead of having to be within arm's reach. Evelyn's elemental water skill was now paired with a growing skill in earth elements. The gardens around the manse had benefited over the past few days as she experimented with her new talents.

Em rose from her seat and put the half-finished tea on the kitchen counter. She felt restless and edgy, and she really just wanted to go home to Boston. There were three more days left of the summit and then they would all go home. Connor would come back to Boston with them for a weekend visit before he headed to New York to work with Thomas on the new PLEA contracts and the investigation into Peter Wolfe. The techs had been examining the devices found at the hotel and there were enough similarities to the ones at the PLEA office attack that they assumed Wolfe was behind the incident. Nothing concrete to take to a judge, but they had enough to prove to themselves it was Wolfe. As she stood by the side window and watched, Edmund used his telekinetics to toss a clay disk into the air and it was either blasted with water from Patrick or a bolt of lightning from Connor or Cullen. All four were gaining impressive control over their new gifts, even with the joking and laughing that went on when the water and lightning hit the disk at the same time and sparks flew like fireworks.

Emlen's attention shifted when Aoife stepped into the room. "Hey Em, you all set?"

The two were going to Cathleen's cottage today to do the ritual to try and break the curse. Em nodded. "I've got the potion in my purse and the spell written out, ready to go. Are you sure your grandma can help with this?"

"Yes, I'm sure," Aoife replied. "I'm not going to put you or the babies at risk. I also called Mira, as you suggested, and she walked Grams and I through the whole thing, so we're good. Come on, I've got the biscuits she wanted and she'll have the tea on for after."

"Alright, let me just tell the guys we're headed out. I'll be taking Liam and Joe as guards today," Em said and opened the side door to step out to the yard. Instead of yelling, she mentally sent to Cullen, "Headed to Cathleen's now. Taking Liam and Joe. I'll call when we're done."

Cullen turned and waved to her, then blew her a kiss before ducking a spray of water from Patrick. Laughter followed Em back inside as she grabbed her purse and joined Aoife out at her car. The two guards followed in one of the SUVs even though it was less than a mile to the cottage. Considering Wolfe knew where they lived, they weren't taking any chances on safety.

Cathleen's cottage was of field stone with window trim and door in bright red and a roof that looked as though it should be thatched instead of shingled. Wild roses and herbs grew in chaotic profusion over stone walls and spilling from garden beds. Neat stone paths led to the front door or around the side to the kitchen entry – which is where Aoife took Em. The autumn chill in the air made the warmth of the wood-fired cook stove welcome when they stepped inside. Wide plank floors and herbs hung from the beamed ceiling showed the age of the house, but the shiny black modern appliances reminded one of the current century.

"Grams, I brought the biscuits...and Emlen," Aoife called into the house.

"I'll be right there," Cathleen called back. "Make yourselves at home."

They sat by the stove in a pair of mismatched upholstered chairs, leaving the rocker for Cathleen. Em's fingers twisted the strap of her purse as nerves roared through her. "I trust Mira, and I trust you, but I'm scared. What if it doesn't work? What if it harms the babies? What if I'm making a mistake?"

"What if you don't do it and it does work?" Cathleen said as she entered the room. "You told me before, you would do anything to make the lives of your children better, yes? This is one of those things. Worst case, it doesn't work. There is no harm that the potion can cause, nor the magic. The ingredients are not dangerous for a pregnant woman, and the magic is subtle and strong."

Emlen let out a breath. "You're right. I'm just freaking out over nothing." She opened her purse and handed the vial to Cathleen, then the paper with the spell on it.

"Are we doing it in the circle?" Aoife asked.

"No, no need. The magic is contained in the potion. The spell is just to activate it. Em drinks the potion, we all recite the spell and that's it," Cathleen replied.

"And we won't even know if it worked until my kids are born. Then Mira can check and see if the curse is still in their blood," Emlen said.

"She can't check yours?" Aoife said.

"No, not really. I don't have any siblings to activate the curse, so it would be hard to tell." Emlen thought for a moment about the little boy Elise had been carrying when she was killed.

"Well, ladies. Let's get on with it then," Cathleen said. Aoife and Cathleen stood on either side of the chair Emlen sat in, each holding copies of the spell. Em opened the vial and took a breath before downing the potion. Once the bottle was empty, Cathleen handed Em her copy and the three started to read in unison. Emlen's mouth tasted like flowers, herbs and something oily, but she still managed to repeat the spell three times with the others. Once they were done, they looked at each other.

Emlen shrugged. "I can't tell if it worked or not, but I could really use some water to wash this taste out of my mouth."

Cathleen chuckled and headed to the stove. "I've had the kettle on for tea and I made some fresh lemonade. Both will go well with the biscuits Aoife brought."

"Lemonade, please," Emlen said. "I'm done with tea for the day. Had two cups already this morning."

"Tea for me, please, Grams," Aoife said. "I'll put the biscuits on a plate." A selection of cookies and the drinks were put on the table as they took their seats.

"Thank you for helping me with this," Emlen told them both. "I just hope it works. Mira is beyond gifted and worked hard to get this potion and spell." A hand rested on her belly. "I would like to know that these two and any siblings they have will have a solid chance at having families and surviving adulthood. It's scary to think I could have missed this if I had a sibling or two."

"I was lucky. I had nine pregnancies and seven healthy births. Even without a curse, motherhood has risks and heartache," Cathleen said, pouring lemonade and tea for them.

"My Mom was a twin," Aoife explained. "Her twin sister died shortly after birth. And there was a stillbirth, right, Grams?"

Cathleen nodded. "My second child was stillborn at eight months. He stopped moving and I went into labor a couple of days later. He's buried with his sister and my husband up beside the church."

Emlen reached out a hand to rest on Cathleen's arm. "Then I'm even more grateful for your help. I'm sure it's not easy, bringing all that back up."

"Oh, it's not that, child," Cathleen said. "The pain of their loss has dulled over the years. I still wonder what kind of people they might have become, but it's not as heart-wrenching as it once was."

"I'm glad to hear that. I am already so attached to these two. I can't fathom what it would be like to lose them, even now," Emlen said.

They talked about children, magic, and the differences between Ireland and America, made promises to visit each other and then Emlen left, leaving Aoife with her grandmother. She got into the SUV with the guards and leaned back with a sigh.

"How'd it go, ma'am?" Liam asked.

"We'll find out in a few months, I guess. Can't tell until the kids are born, then Mira can check and see if the curse is present."

"Well, here's hoping all ends well," Liam said.

"Here's hoping," Emlen replied.

Cullen and Connor were sitting in the side garden at a table, bottles of water in their hands.

"Well, this is a twist we weren't expecting, huh?" Connor said. "I guess we should've expected some kind of magic to show up, but wouldn't it have been when we were kids?"

"Maybe it sort of did," Cullen replied. "I mean, remember how we used to always give each other shocks and we didn't even have to rub our socks on the carpet?"

Connor snorted laughter. "Yeah, Mom yelled at us for blowing light bulbs all the time and popping fuses. Then we grew out of it or something."

Cullen just stared at him, then arched a brow, "Or something."

Realization spread across Connor's face. "Ohh."

"Yeah, oh," Cullen replied. "We probably shut it down ourselves. It wasn't hugely powerful, and we didn't know, so it phased out as we grew. At least, that's what Edmund was saying."

"How weird is it that we're friends with – and you're now related to – the President of the United States? And his husband?" Connor shook his head, chuckling. "And the Chief Justice of the Supreme Court is making potions for your wife and twin babies?"

"Gawd, I know. Twins. What the hell am I going to do with twins?"

"Raise them as well as our parents raised us."

"At least I have an amazing woman at my side to help me, like Dad did. That makes me a lot less terrified. Not much, but a bit less terrified."

Connor laughed and toasted his brother with his water bottle. A few minutes of silence, then Connor spoke up once more. "Cull, what are you going to do when we get back to Boston?"

"Help Em set up the house for the babies and keep doing what I can for PLEA."

"Well, I have a job for you in Boston. If you want it. But...you'll need to carry a gun." Connor watched his brother's face as he spoke.

"No," Cullen said. "I won't ever carry again."

"Cull, I need..."

"No, Connor. Stop. You know why I can't."

"No, I know why you won't, but I still think you're wrong. You weren't responsible for Hendry's death."

"You weren't there, Connor. You don't know."

"I know that you were well-trained and skilled as an officer. You told me what happened and I don't see how you could have done more. There were two of you and five of them. They had assault weapons and you two had Glocks. The firepower alone counted against you. Add in the ambush and you're just lucky you didn't die with him. Look, Cullen, you can second-guess and what-if yourself into insanity all day long, but it isn't going to change the facts. Hendry took several rounds across his thighs, hitting both femoral arteries. Even if a paramedic had been in the back seat with you, he would have bled out before you could get him to help."

"Shut up, Connor. I'm done talking about it. I'm not carrying again on the job and I'm not going to be a cop again."

"I'm not asking you to be a cop, Cullen. I'm asking you to be my partner in PLEA. My co-President. But in order to be a member of PLEA, you need to carry a gun and keep up your training. What would you do if someone came after Emlen or your children? Chase them with a baseball bat? Mace? A taser? Come on, man. Be reasonable! I mean, seriously, Cullen. You seem to actively go against your training and instincts, acting less and less like a trained cop as time goes on."

Cullen went still when Connor brought up Em and the babies. He hadn't thought about all of the aspects of his decision. In his heart, he knew he'd always put his wife and children first, but what if he couldn't? "Connor, what if I can't carry? What if I hold a gun and can't fire it? What if I lose Em or the babies because I freeze up?"

"Cull, you refused the psychotherapist. I think it's time to actually talk to one. The one that we have with PLEA is fantastic and understands magic users too. They can help you work through this." Connor paused a moment and then spoke quietly. "They helped me."

Cullen looked up at his brother. "What?"

"They helped me. When I saw you at the hospital, covered in blood, I almost quit the force too. I couldn't process what I would have done if I had lost you that night. You took a bullet in the shoulder and you were damned lucky it didn't kill you. I hugged you and spent the rest of the night staring at your blood on my hands. I wouldn't wash it off for hours.

I kept thinking it was the last time I would have touched you."

"Jeezus, Connor. I had no idea."

"And I wanted it that way. You had enough to deal with. You didn't need to be dealing with my mental breakdown on top of it all. Jeanine is the therapist I saw back then and it turns out she was part of the Garda. So when everything was being transitioned, I asked her if she'd come work for PLEA and she did."

Cullen looked up at his brother, the water bottle twisted in his fingers. "Alright, I'll do it. I'll talk to Jeanine and I'll take the job as your co-President. I appreciate you wanting me at your side, Connor." Hand outstretched, Cullen waited for Connor to shake.

Instead, Connor rose to his feet, came around the table and tugged his brother up out of his own seat and into a hug. "I love you, brother. I'm glad you're coming back to where you belong."

Cullen hugged Connor back and grinned. "Love ya too, punk. Come on, let's go tell Em and see if Joel's around so we can tell him he's finally getting what he wanted."

Connor smirked as he shoulder-bumped Cull. "Still don't know how she puts up with you."

"Me neither," Cullen replied. "Me neither."

Chapter Fourteen

On the private jet, the trip back was a bit different than the one to Dublin. Ryan's ashes were in an urn, packed with the luggage while his ghost hung out with the team. Kian was still in Ireland for a few months until he could be judged safe to fly home for more rehab. He was healing and working hard to be ready for the fancy prosthetics PLEA promised him. Everyone had expected to stop in New York and drop off Connor and his assistant before heading on to Boston, but Edmund had sent a message asking them to come to DC for a few days first. He wouldn't expand on why he needed them there, but when the President asks, one does their best to make it happen.

Emlen curled up against Cullen and fell asleep for most of the trip. He gently nudged her awake when the captain announced the approach to Andrews. "Buckle up, love. We're about to land," Cullen said. Emlen's fingers fumbled with the buckle for a moment before it clicked and she settled back in the seat.

Cull handed her a warm washcloth and she used it to wipe the sleep from her eyes and clean her hands. "I wonder what happened that Edmund couldn't tell us over the SAT phone or through the classified servers. I'm wondering if it has something to do with JJ," Emlen said. "I dreamt that JJ was out and causing trouble – okay, had a nightmare that he was out."

Cullen reached for her hand and gave it a light squeeze. "If JJ got out, PLEA would have been alerted."

"True. Okay, that helps," Em said, gaze settled on Connor across from them. "I'm glad you're working with Connor again and doing something you love." She lifted Cullen's hand, still clasped in hers, and kissed his fingers. "Having something that challenges and fulfills you is important. Something outside of what you and I share."

"Knowing I've got a secure position for as long as I want it, helps. I will admit I was wondering how I would be able to effectively contribute when the kids got here." Cullen raised a hand to stop her from interrupting. "Yes, I know you're an heiress and neither one of us needs to work, but I was raised to take care of myself and my family. I need to feel I'm doing my part – and this position with PLEA allows me to do that."

"I understand," Emlen said. "And I'm also glad that it's forced you to make the changes you needed in order to heal. I need a healthy, stable partner to raise these magical twins we're about to have."

Cullen leaned in to kiss her, hand caressing her belly. "You, and they, deserve the best and I'll do what I can to deliver that."

The plane bumped to a stop and the crew bustled about. Once all the belongings were collected and the door opened, a pair of Secret Service agents boarded, showing their ID. "Ambassador O'Brien, Mr. and Mrs. O'Brien, the President has sent an escort to bring you to the White House by helicopter. The rest of your entourage will be driven to Mayfield. After your meeting and dinner at the White House, you are all invited to stay at Mayfield until you depart for home. Is that acceptable?" The three

O'Briens nodded and took a minute to shuffle papers and bags so they had everything they needed.

Emlen made sure Ryan's ashes would be secured at Mayfield, and the three moved to follow the agents down the stairs and across the tarmac to the waiting copter. Conversation was minimal during the ride, even with headsets, with everyone wondering what warranted this level of rush and secrecy. They landed on the White House lawn and took golf carts to the residence entrance.

Edmund and Patrick were waiting with hugs and refreshments, not addressing the reason for their presence until the agents had left the room. Emlen sat her cup of coffee down and gave Edmund a look. "President or no, you're still my uncle and I'm telling you, this unplanned side trip has us all imagining the worst. What the hell is going on?" Tina shimmered into visibility in the room and gave Emlen a smile.

"Hey, Em. Glad you're back." Before Em could say a thing, Edmund looked at Tina.

"Hello, Tina." Everyone went silent except for Tina, who chuckled. "Yeah, he can see me."

"Um," Emlen started. "It seems Edmund can see ghosts now, too." Em shook her head and turned to Edmund. "Okay, you can see ghosts. But why has that warranted us coming here instead of you just letting us know?"

Cullen and Connor both moved their chairs closer so they could touch Em and hear Tina.

"Because of what I told him," Tina said. "JJ has been writing letters, but not mailing them. Yet, they're disappearing from his room and replies are appearing. Someone is using magic to communicate with him. He writes something, puts it in a clay jar and sets the lid on top. The next day he opens the jar and pulls out a different letter."

"Well, hell," Emlen muttered. "Did you see who was writing to him?"

Tina nodded, "The only thing I saw was the name "Peter"."

"Peter Wolfe," Connor said.

"Who is Peter Wolfe?" Tina asked.

"The man responsible for the attacks we've suffered while in Dublin," Cullen replied.

"And the man responsible for the E street explosion here in DC," Patrick added.

"Whomever he is, he has a real hatred for both the Order and the Garda, or PLEA now."

"Well, magic or no magic, if he's writing letters, he has to touch the paper, correct? Prints are prints. I think it's time we grabbed one of those letters and found out who this Wolfe really is," Connor said.

"Cullen and I can go visit him and while I'm talking to him, Cullen can grab a letter," Emlen said.

"That's probably the easiest way to do it. Bring Tina and he can talk to her again. It will keep him engrossed enough that I could toss his whole room and he wouldn't notice," Cullen said.

Emlen looked to Tina. "You okay with that?"

"Sure. After being around him all this time with no way to smack him for his stupidity, I'd love to be able to actually connect for a few," Tina said.

Patrick chuckled, "Don't bloody him too much. They'd blame Em and Cull."

"Hell, I'll take the blame if you break his nose," Cullen muttered.

"Yeah, let's not. I don't want to give birth in prison," Emlen retorted and everyone chuckled.

"Okay, so what is the procedure for going to visit?" Connor asked. "I've already told them to expect a visit from family tomorrow morning. That way we can have dinner and you can go to Mayfield and rest. The facility is closer to Mayfield than here, that's why I'm not asking you to stay here," Edmund said.

"Food sounds great. I'm starving," Em said and Cullen laughed. "Well, you are eating for three."

"Wait…three?" Edmund stared at Emlen. "You're carrying twins?"

"Yes, a boy and a girl," Emlen said. "Well, congratulations. Now put your feet up and I'll let the chef know we'll be eating in the dining room up here so you don't have to walk too far. Do you need some water?" Edmund started to fuss and the others laughed.

"Relax, Edmund. I'm perfectly healthy, just a little tired from the flight. I'd like to wash up and brush my hair before we sit down for dinner, if that's okay?"

"Of course, of course. I'll just…" Edmund trailed off.

Patrick gave him a hug, saying. "Breathe, she's not having the babies now and she's fine. We'll soon have two to spoil, so start shopping. I'll show her where the bathroom is located."

"Thanks, Pat," Em said as she got to her feet and grabbed her purse. Soon they were all seated around the cozy table in the family quarters. Cozy for the White House residence sat ten people in a room decorated with some of Edmund and Patrick's things mixed with White House antiques and treasures.

Emlen couldn't stop looking around the room until the first course was served and the scent of the rich soup reminded her how hungry she was. "I can't get over how beautiful this place is. Isn't it weird, living in a museum?" Em asked.

"It feels like home most of the time, but sometimes it catches me up and I realize I'm living in the same house Lincoln lived in. Then it's weird," Patrick said.

"Now that I can see them, it gets to me when I'm walking down a hallway and Willie Lincoln's ghost jumps out at me. Or President Harrison, President Taylor or Mrs. Wilson start a conversation while I'm on a conference call. Harrison's the worst for that. He'll just start talking and I have to mute my phone and ask him to please wait because I'm speaking to others. He doesn't understand because he can't see anyone else in the room," Edmund said.

"Oh, right. Because he died before the telephone was invented. He died in 1841 and Bell got the first patent in the 1870's," Connor said.

"My brother, the purveyor of random facts," Cullen teased.

"That's the truth, though," Edmund said. "When I explained to Harrison how the phone worked, he kept trying to look under the desk for the people I was speaking to. It would have been funny if I weren't trying to talk to eight people and two interpreters."

Laughter and good food filled the evening and soon the travelers were settled back at Mayfield, sleeping the sleep of the jet lagged.

The trip to the facility where JJ was living took only about twenty minutes from Mayfield. He'd been moved, for security reasons, to a private location with enhanced protection provided by PLEA and the Secret Service. What had once been a retreat for a rich family now held a selection of cottages where the staff and their patient lived in pastoral comfort. They were checked through the gate and wound up the mile long drive to eventually stop at a stone house with a dark green metal roof. Faint smoke curled from a chimney at one end and wide windows boasted dark green shutters and white trim. A covered porch held a pair of wicker chairs beside a table and a few potted plants. The guard standing under the porch overhang at the top of the stairs disrupted the image of domestic bliss.

Cullen helped Em out of the car, then nodded to the guard. The agents that came with them stepped up onto the porch and spoke to the guard before one moved to the other side of the porch entrance. Another opened the door and went inside while a third walked around the back of the building and took a position at the back door. The one inside came back out and nodded to Cullen and Emlen, and only then did they go up the steps and into the house. The furnishings were simple and comfortable, fitted to the country cottage theme without being overly feminine.

JJ sat on the sofa until he saw Emlen come in and then he leaped to his feet. "Emmy, oh I'm so happy to see you," JJ moved to give her a hug and Em stepped back.

"No, I don't think so," Emlen said.

JJ kept moving forward and Cullen stepped in his path.

"My wife said no. Back off."

JJ smirked. "Wife. Right. You married her the same day my brother in law married his pet."

Emlen stepped around Cullen and slapped JJ in the face. The agent stepped one pace towards them and Cullen waved him back. "I think she's done."

JJ snarled and stepped back. "If she touches me again, shoot her."

"Yeah, that's not going to happen. The shooting, I mean," Emlen said as she reached out and grabbed his arm.

Tina stepped up to JJ and smacked him in the back of the head so hard his head snapped forward. "What the actual fuck, Johnny? Are you completely off the rails?" Tina screamed at him. "She's carrying your goddamned grandchildren and you're going to threaten to shoot her?"

"Grandchildren, plural?" JJ said and then he laughed. "Figures. Bitch is going to have a litter."

Cullen snarled and reached for JJ, but Emlen pushed him back. "Don't, he's not worth it." She kept her hand on JJ's arm and pushed him down to the couch. "Sit there and do yourself a favor and only speak when spoken to."

Em then perched on the arm of the chair and looked up at Tina. "Okay, you've been haunting this dickhead since he lost his mind in the State of the Union Address, now's your chance to say all the things you've been holding back."

"Wait, she's been following me since then?" JJ started to get up and Em pushed him back down.

"Sit there and behave or I'll have the agents handcuff you to a chair for this."

"You can't treat me like this. I am your fath..." Emlen lifted a finger and arched a brow.

"Yeah, don't try that one on me."

"You can't treat me like this, I was the President."

"Yeah, you were. Because you murdered the last one. Then you went crazy, so yeah, shut up." Tina said. "Unless I'm asking you to answer a question."

The agent snorted a soft sound of laughter, then calmed himself when Em gave him a look. Cullen left the room and went into the bathroom. Once he was certain JJ was focused on Tina, he slipped out and went into the bedroom. The clay jar was on a bookcase and he went right to it and opened it. Inside was a folded up letter, so Cullen grabbed his handkerchief and reached in to pull the letter out. A shake of his hand opened the paper enough to see that it was a letter to JJ.

He sealed it in a baggie, put it in his pocket, then closed the jar. He spent a few more minutes searching and found a stack of letters under the mattress. He used the handkerchief to pick up the whole stack and there were a lot of them. Too many to stuff into the baggies he had with him.

Instead, he took a hand towel out of the bathroom and folded the letters up in it, then stuck them under his shirt in his waistband. Back in the bathroom, he flushed the toilet and ran some water, then came back out.

Cullen gave Emlen a thumbs up and stepped out of the house. Back at the SUV, he got the agent standing near the vehicle to take custody of the towel-wrapped letters and put them in a sealed bag, then took the sealed one and wrote the time, date, and case info on both. Chain of custody was crucial in any case and Cullen didn't want to damage the letters by sweating on them.

Tina paced back and forth in front of JJ, fingers curled into fists. "I want to just keep hitting you until you get brain damage that might make you a decent human being again, but I know things don't work that way."

"And that would make you more like him. Not worth it," Em said.

"I never beat up a woman," JJ started. "I always treated..."

"No, you paid someone to kill your pregnant wife and unborn son. You paid someone to try and kill Emlen when she was a toddler and ended up killing her mother. You've killed more people than I can keep track of and you want to argue that you never personally hit a woman so it's okay?" Tina would've been spitting in his face if she were alive, her fury putting her within inches of his nose.

JJ lifted a hand and Emlen lifted hers so Tina disappeared.

"Watch yourself, asshole," Emlen warned him. "Tina, step back." After a moment, Em put her hand back on JJ's shoulder. "Try that again, JJ, and this conversation is over."

Tina was across the room, arms folded under her breasts. She glared at JJ and then started to speak. "You stinking piece of shit that once was my brother. Tell us about Peter Wolfe."

JJ's expression went from antagonistic and cocky to pale and terrified the moment he heard that name. "Wh...who?"

"Peter Wolfe. You know, the guy you've been exchanging letters with for however long," Emlen said.

"I don't get mail here. Not that isn't checked by the guards and such first. I'm not allowed."

"Right," Em said, then turned to the agent. "Go get it."

The agent turned and went into JJ's room, then came out with the clay jar. "Care to revise your statement?" Em asked.

"That's just some decorative thing. What are you talking about?" JJ said.

"Oh, so it'd be okay if the agent over there dropped it?" Tina said.

"No, it's probably an antique. Don't drop it," JJ turned to look at the agent. "Just put it back."

"Naw, I think it would look great in my den. Since you're family and all, I think I'll take it home. Hand it over to the agent outside to put in the car, would you?" Em said.

The agent walked toward the door and JJ bolted to his feet. Em grabbed his hair and jerked him back around, shoving him face-first into the sofa, a knee in his lower back. "Bring your cuffs over here, would you?" she asked the agent.

He set the jar on a table and brought his cuffs over, fastening JJ's hands behind his back before propping him back upright on the couch. JJ was cursing and spluttering the whole time until the agent put his hand on his gun and glared at him. Only then did JJ quiet down.

"Smart man," Emlen said, voice low. "You're only alive on my tolerance right now, so I suggest you answer the questions. Who is Peter Wolfe?" The agent handed the jar out the door to the other agent who set it into a bubble-wrap lined box and put that box inside a lead lined case in the back of the SUV. JJ looked from Emlen to Tina and started giggling.

The giggling turned into full-blown laughter before Tina moved closer and slapped his face. "Johnny, snap out of it. Who is this guy?"

Tears from the laughter were running down JJ's face as he coughed out. "Brian. He's your beloved Brian." Tina looked horrified and then angry. "That's not funny, Johnny. Brian was killed. I saw him in the car when it blew up."

"Oh, he was in it alright, but he survived. He is Peter Wolfe."

Tina sat down on the side chair and covered her face with her hands. "Oh. My. Gods."

Emlen let go of JJ and went over to Tina, crouching before her and putting her hands on Tina's knees. "Auntie, tell me. Who is this guy?"

JJ kept giggling on the couch and the agent moved to stand behind him where he could keep him from getting up if necessary.

Tina's voice was soft and ragged as she spoke. "Brian Peters. He was my garda for over five years. We were in love and he asked me to marry him."

"What happened?"

"Daddy happened," JJ said. "Peters was Garda. That was not good enough for his baby girl. He didn't know about them, but I did. I told him. So he had him killed."

"You fucking bastard!" Tina roared and launched herself at JJ. To be honest, Emlen didn't know if it was the boost in her powers, the power of the babies, or the sheer pain and fury that Tina felt at that moment – but Tina launched herself at JJ and physically rocked him back on the couch. Em had fallen backwards and it took her a moment to get to her feet, but by then the damage was done. Tina's hand was inside JJ's chest and his face went gray, lips turned blue as he gasped. The agent tried to help but there was nothing for him to grab onto.

When Emlen finally got her hands on Tina and pulled her back, JJ was dead. Tina had crushed his heart, just as he had broken hers so many years before.

Chapter Fifteen

"In other news, President John Frederick Jackson's funeral was kept private followed by interment at Arlington National Cemetery. The final conclusion on the cause of death was heart failure from a previously undiagnosed defect."

Emlen turned the television off and tossed the remote onto the table. "Heart failure. That's one way of putting it."

"Well, his heart failed to continue pumping after his dead sister crushed it, so it's not a lie," Joel said.

"Very funny. Not," Emlen said. "I didn't like watching my aunt kill my father. Granted, the bastard got what he deserved, but I'd rather not have seen it happen."

"Has his ghost shown up yet?" Joel asked.

"Not yet. I'm hoping it got sucked right into hell," Emlen replied. "Have you seen Tina?"

"She's been scarce. I think she's still processing everything. I did tell her that she shouldn't feel guilty for killing him. He wouldn't have stopped and according to the letters we found, he was feeding Wolfe info that helped him track down where we were in Ireland and here. The brothers have beefed up security at Mayfield, but we're all heading to Boston and New York tomorrow, now that the funeral and investigation are over."

"What about the O'Briens in Boston?"

"A PLEA contingent was sent up the day after he died to help with security at the manse. There were a couple of incidents of pro-Jackson supporters throwing rocks and spray painting the fence, but that was handled quickly and quietly. Scatha is up there and I can't wait to see him. I miss my feathered friend."

"I'm sure he misses you too. I haven't seen Simone since your wedding. Do you think she crossed over?"

"I hope she did. I think she felt responsible for JJ's behavior and the shame kept her from being around us."

"His behavior is not on her, it's his father's fault. That man poisoned his son and destroyed his life."

"I agree. I just hope I can do well by these two." Em's hand rested on her belly, sensing the satisfied emotions of her babies.

"How are you doing? Feeling rested enough?" Joel stepped closer and then asked in a near whisper, "May I touch?"

Emlen smiled at him and nodded. His hand settled on the curve of her belly and a gentle thump brushed his palm. "Oh, my stars. Hello, little one. I'm your Uncle Joel."

Tears pricked Emlen's eyes but she blinked them away, not wanting to upset Joel. "That was the boy. The girl is here," Emlen slid his hand to the side and he was rewarded with another thump. "I think they like your voice."

"Have you come up with names yet?"

"We're tossing around a few. I think we need to meet them first, then we'll know."

"And what happens if they tell you they don't like the names you choose?"

Emlen stared at Joel for a moment, then started laughing. "You're mean. They're going to love their names and their family."

Joel laughed with her and gave her a hug. "You're going to make an amazing mother. Enjoy every moment, little one."

"Who's got you laughing?" Cullen asked as he came into the room.

"Joel's here," Em said and reached for Cull's hand so he could see him too.

"Hey, Joel, how's things?" Cullen asked.

"Things is good, boyo. Was just getting a chance to say hello to your offspring."

"Yeah, the kids thumped his hand to say hi. It was adorable."

"Aww, that's cute. Hope they can see him because we're going to need babysitters," Cullen teased.

"Oh, we'll have plenty of babysitters," Emlen said, "between dead and living grandparents, uncles, aunts, and cousins."

"Speaking of which, has JJ's ghost shown up?" Cullen asked.

"No, thank gods. I don't want to see him again. If he did show up, I don't know how to get rid of him," Emlen said.

"I do. Ryan and I went by the PLEA offices before you all left Dublin. There were three confused spirits wandering around and getting violent with investigators. We each grabbed an arm, told them they were done, and pulled them to the Between place. They didn't have anyone that wanted them back, so they stayed. Since the only person with a tie to JJ on this side is you, if he shows up, Ryan and I can pull him over," Joel said.

"Oh, good," Emlen sighed. "That makes me feel a little better." She turned to Cullen, "Are we almost ready to go?"

"Except for the last few things we'll need tonight and in the morning, everything's packed, so yeah, we're ready to go."

"I'm glad. I want to get home."

"Me too," Cullen replied. "Feels like forever since we've been back in Boston."

Joel stepped up and patted Cullen's shoulder, "I'll get out of your hair tonight and go help keep watch. Ryan's already out there." He paused and leaned over to Em, "I'll also see if Simone has crossed over and check on Tina."

"Thanks, Joel. I'd appreciate you doing that. I'm worried about Tina, and want to thank her," Em said.

"I'll let her know," Joel said and faded out. Emlen turned to Cullen and pulled him down for a kiss. "How about a quiet dinner, just the two of us, and an early night? I'd like some husband and wife time with you."

"Now you're talking," Cullen smiled and kissed her back. "I'll take care of ordering dinner and you clear the table in our room. Anything you're in the mood for?"

"Anything that doesn't have tomato sauce. It's been giving me heartburn the last few times."

"You got it."

Dinner had been over for a while and the two were cuddled up in bed, talking quietly. The sound of a cleared throat made Cullen reach for the light. Emlen kept a hand on his arm and they blinked at Tina who stood at the foot of their bed.

"Uh, Tina? What's up?" Emlen asked.

Cullen slid his arm around Em and gave Tina a warm smile. "It's okay, Tina. We were just talking. Planned an early night of it since we're all headed back to Boston tomorrow."

"I'm a horrible person," Tina whispered. "I killed my baby brother."

"Oh, Tina, no. You're not horrible. Did Joel tell you I wanted to see you?" Emlen asked.

Tina nodded, arms wrapped around herself, head bowed.

"I wanted to see you to thank you. We found out from the letters that JJ had been feeding Peter information about all of us. They planned on having everyone killed, including me and the babies."

Tina's head snapped up and her eyes blazed. "They better not touch those babies!"

Cullen nodded, "That's pretty much how I feel about it too. So you did us a favor, Tina. You saved the babies and all of us."

Tina brightened up after hearing Cullen's words and seeing Emlen nod in agreement. "Okay, I can see that. Thank you."

"So, Tina," Em said. "What can you tell us about Peters?"

"Brian was a sweet guy. Considerate, caring, professional... he was an excellent Garda. He said he fell in love with me a year after starting as my Garda and kept it professional the whole time. It wasn't until that last year that we started actually dating and having a romance."

"And then what happened?" Cullen asked.

"We were going to elope. We were in his car, heading into town for the ceremony when Simmons rear-ended us. Brian kept driving and floored it. Simmons and Dunleavy were in an SUV behind us and kept bumping the rear corners of our car, trying to force us off the road.

We pulled up to a railroad crossing, the bars were down and Brian took a look up the tracks and floored it. Smashed right through the bars and across the tracks. The train clipped the back of the car and sent it spinning out of control. It slammed into a metal pole on the driver's side. Brian was okay, but the doors were pinned. He smashed the rest of the windshield and shoved me out. I got away from the car and sat by a tree, I was shaking so hard and I'd hit my head. Brian got out, then turned to dive back in to grab something." Tina took a breath and closed her eyes before continuing. "The car blew up. Simmons and Dunleavy crossed after the train and grabbed me up and stuffed me into the SUV and drove away. When they pulled up at the mansion, I got out and ran, and that's when Simmons shot and killed me."

Emlen got out of bed and went over to Tina, wrapping her in a hug. "Oh, Tina. That's so awful. I'm so sorry." She led her over to the bed and sat down, taking Cullen's hand once more so he could see and hear Tina again.

"I'm sorry, Tina. Em's right, that's horrible," Cullen said, voice low. "If that's the case, how did Pete...er, Brian survive?"

"I have no idea. Maybe someone pulled him free. I'd love to be able to talk to him, but it sounds like he's gone off the deep end like Johnny did."

"And if you were going to actually talk to him, I'd have to be there," Emlen said. "And I'm not so sure that's a good idea. Not with how much he wants us all dead."

"No," Tina said. "The risk to you and the twins is not worth it."

"Maybe we can put a letter in the jar and see what happens?" Cullen said.

"Now that's a brilliant idea," Emlen replied. "Let's do that. Tina, can you dictate a letter and I'll write it and sign it as you?"

"Yeah, this could work. I can talk about things only he and I would know," Tina said, thinking carefully about what to write to her once-lover.

A clock chimed downstairs and Emlen yawned. "Okay, let's do the letter thing once we get to Boston. I need to sleep and we're traveling tomorrow. Another day isn't going to make much of a difference at this point, right?"

"Right. We'll deal with it once we get home," Cullen said.

"Gives me time to figure out what I want to say. I'll see you guys later," Tina said and faded out of the room.

Chapter Sixteen

They'd spent two days in New York City with Connor, arranging Cullen's appointments with Jeanine Markam, the psychotherapist Connor had working with PLEA, for those days each month she would be in Boston. Meals were had either at the UN offices of PLEA or nearby, but the last night they had dinner at Connor's townhouse. The place used to be Garda property and while they'd sold off or repurposed most of the Garda assets, they had kept a few, including this place a few short miles from the UN. Four bedrooms, five baths, Connor kept his own suite of rooms private and shared the place with Thomas and Evelyn whenever they were in town as well as guest rooms for visiting PLEA officials. Saved the organization a fortune in hotel and rental fees.

The formal granting of Cullen's new title and position had been that evening with Thomas in attendance and now the four friends sat around the table, laughing over Thomas' tales of how he fumbled when first learning his powers.

Cullen had been so nervous when he went up to the mic for his acceptance speech, his powers sparked and shorted out the sound system. Now Connor was calling him "Sparky" and the two were making electricity dance across their fingertips.

"Okay, boys. Put the lightning back in the bottle. The kids are getting jumpy," Emlen said, hands smoothing over her belly as the twins shifted and thumped beneath her hands.

Connor leaned over and held out his hand, asking with a look if he could touch. Emlen smiled and nodded, taking his hand to rest over the spot where both were thumping.

"Hey little ones. It's me, your Uncle Connor. Sorry we got you all excited. Need you to settle down now so your mommy can sleep soon. Can you do that for me? Settle down a bit?"

Almost as if they understood him, the babies settled and Emlen let out a slow breath. "Thank you. They're getting so active I find myself standing by the dishwasher so the sound lulls them to sleep."

Connor leaned over and kissed her blouse-covered belly. "Sleep well, little ones. We'll get to meet soon." Then he leaned up and kissed Emlen's cheek. "Go rest, sister-mine. Your flight leaves early tomorrow because we need the plane back that afternoon to get Thomas home."

Em kissed Connor's cheek in return and hugged him before patting Thomas' shoulder and smiling at Cullen. "You stay and visit. I'm going to go enjoy that fancy shower with all the shower heads and then sleep."

Cullen got up to give her a kiss and walked her to their room before coming back to enjoy whiskey and cigars in the study with Thomas and Connor. A very early morning flight landed them in Boston without incident and a drive to the manse that took a while due to commuter traffic had them home for the first time in months.

When they pulled into the drive at the manse, Emlen felt the tension slide away. "I have missed this place."

"I've missed it too, and I'm eager to see my folks," Cullen replied. They'd barely got out of the car before Scatha was perched on Emlen's shoulder, rubbing his head against her cheek. Thanks to the leitung, Cullen could still hear her familiar as he greeted them.

~It has been too long. You've both been missed. Wait, your magic – it's much stronger. What happened?~

"It's a long story, Scatha. Let's get inside and get settled and we'll fill everyone in," Cullen said.

~And you have magic. Yes, much to discuss. Hello, little ones. Yes, I hear you.~

"You're talking to the babies already?" Emlen asked, giving the bird a sideways look.

~Why not? They're talking to me. Not words like you do, but images and emotions. They say you understand them, so why should it be different for me?~

"Because you're a bird?" Cullen teased as he carried a bag and opened the door for Emlen. The agents would unload the rest while they went to see Eileen and James.

~I may be a bird, but I'm a Familiar and far from ordinary.~ Scatha preened and fluttered his wings.

"Yes, yes, you're awesome," Emlen assured him before she turned and was wrapped into a hug from Eileen. Scatha fluttered off Em's shoulder and settled on the top of an open door.

"You're finally home. Oh, look at how big those babies are getting. Come here, get off your feet. We've got lunch ready and..." Eileen bustled about, fussing over Em.

Cullen derailed his mom when he wrapped his arms around her and hugged her from behind. "Mom, settle down. We're here now and not going anywhere for a good while. The babies will be born right here in town and this is home base. Just breathe."

Eileen swatted his arm. "I'm just excited. Let me go so I can tell Mrs. A you're here."

James stepped into the space Eileen left and hugged first Emlen, then Cullen. "Glad you're home safe. Your mother's been in a tizzy." He leaned over and whispered "She's been having nightmares. Won't talk to me about them."

Cullen frowned, "Any ideas?"

"Normal nightmares or magical ones?" Emlen asked.

"No, no ideas and I don't know, Em. Maybe you can get her to tell you what's going on," James said.

"I'll talk to her later in private and see what she says," Emlen replied.

"Come settle in the dining room. Mrs. A is bringing the food," Eileen called out.

They set the bags down in the hallway and went in to sit down, Em pausing to hug Mrs. A before she sat. "Missed your cooking, Mrs. A. Thank you for making us lunch."

"Happy to do it, lovey. Glad you're home where you belong. Those babies need to be born here, not in some strange place or country," Mrs. A replied.

"That's the plan, Mrs. A. Settle in, set up the nursery and enjoy being home," Cullen said.

"Good to hear it," Mrs. A said before she returned to the kitchen to get the last of the food.

"I think she missed you more than me, Cullen," Em said as she looked at the food on the table.

"All of your favorites. Fried chicken, mashed potatoes, peas, corn on the cob..."

"And fresh-baked rolls," Mrs. A added as she set the basket on the table with a bowl of butter. "Now dig in, everyone."

The excellent food, good conversation, and being home at last did wonders for both Emlen and Cullen. The agents and Mrs. A's assistant got the luggage inside and sorted into the various rooms and Mrs. A made sure they were all fed. The crew left the family alone in the dining room to reconnect.

Emlen could hear them laughing from the kitchen and sighed. "Feels so good to be here. Now I can relax."

"I know what you mean. I think we just needed to be home," Cullen said.

"Yes, you both needed to be home," Eileen said and reached out to squeeze Em's hand.

"Wait until you see what we brought you back from Ireland," Emlen told her. "You're going to love it. Whiskey for James and something lovely for you."

"You could've just got me whiskey," Eileen teased.

"Well, I'm sure James will share."

"Don't be so sure," James laughed, then winked at Eileen. "Yes, of course I'll share."

"Well, if he doesn't, Cullen bought some too and is going to save a few bottles for when I'm able to partake of alcohol again. In about two years?" Emlen sighed and patted her belly. "I hope you appreciate my sacrifice, little ones."

Everyone chuckled as Eileen passed the rolls over and James leaned back. "If Connor were here, it'd be perfect. I'm so proud of my family."

"Well, it's not the same, but..." Cullen pulled out his phone, dialed Connor, hit speaker and set the phone on the table.

"Yeah, Cull, what's up?" Connor answered. "You're on speaker with me, Em, Ma, and Da. We're having lunch and Da missed you," Cullen said.

"Hey, everyone. This is actually great timing, Cullen. I got the fingerprint results back from the letters."

"Yeah? Any good news?" Cullen asked.

"Not really. The prints are likely Peters', but there's so much scar tissue, it's only a vague match. Yet, knowing what we know about the accident, it would fit. That, and what Jackson told us. The content of the letters seems to fit as well."

"Okay, so we can assume, with minimal risk, that the person Jackson was working with was Peters," Emlen said. "Which we already were assuming but couldn't confirm."

"And still can't without some doubt, but all the pieces fit," Connor said. "Is this about that perp behind the attacks in Ireland?" James asked.

"Yeah, turns out he was working with Jackson, getting intel so he could target us more effectively. They used spelled jars that passed letters back and forth. We never would've known about it if not for Tina," Connor explained. "She really saved us with not only her intel, but with taking out Jackson. Which reminds me, Cullen. Take me off speaker, got some business to discuss. Love you all. Hope to see you for Christmas next week."

"Bye, Connor," rang out from around the table as Cullen tapped the phone and rose to leave the room.

"Okay, brother. What's up?" he asked, leaving the other three to chat and finish lunch as he ducked into the library and shut the door behind him.

"There are more attacks planned. One somewhere here in New York City, one in Boston and one in DC. We're still gathering intel and analyzing the letters, but I think if you can get Tina to write that letter sooner rather than later, it'd be good. We need to shake this guy up and see if we can stop these attacks."

"Shit, well, yeah. Okay, if not tonight then tomorrow, I'll get Em to sit with Tina and write it up. Did the case and jar get delivered here already?"

"Yeah, Amos signed for it. It should be in the safe room. That's where I told him to store it."

"Sounds good. I'll track it down while Em's napping and make sure it's ready to roll."

"Cull, this guy is doing all of this to make people pay for, and I quote, "his beloved Valentina's death". That means while he may be highly intelligent, he's acting on powerful emotion and loss. Maybe knowing that can help with how the letter is written. Good luck, and let me know how it goes?"

"Will do, little brother. Love you."

"Love you, too. Bye."

Cullen hung up the call and leaned his hips against the desk, gaze on the window across the room and the faint tease of snowflakes against the gray sky. He really hoped they could get this mess with Peters settled soon. He didn't want to be worrying about mad bombers when he needed to focus on his wife and impending fatherhood.

Em tapped on the door, then stepped inside at his call to enter. She moved to wrap her arms around him and rested her head on his chest. "I'm going to go up and rest for a bit. Your folks are going to watch a movie in the living room since the forecast is for a lot more snow today."

Cullen wrapped his arms around her and kissed the top of her head. "Go rest, love. I've got some stuff to check out for Connor. When you're awake, let me know? We need to talk to Tina about the letter."

"Okay, love," Emlen yawned, then reached up to kiss his jaw. "See you in a bit."

He watched her leave the room and smiled. If anyone had told him a year ago that this would be his life, he would've laughed. Now, he just counted himself blessed.

Chapter Seventeen

Emlen, Tina, and Eileen sat in the library at the table. A fire burned on the hearth, adding welcome heat to the room. One of Mrs. A's tea trays sat at the end of the table with cups, plates, and crumbs scattered among the notebook and papers. Em had a hand on Eileen's leg while Tina dictated a letter that Eileen was writing. She had wanted to help and her handwriting was better than Em's so they'd agreed.

"End it with, 'Brian, if this is you, please stop hurting my friends and family. This isn't going to do anything but make me hate you. I may be a ghost, but you're still alive and you have a chance to make things better for people, not worse. The man I love would want things to be better. Love always, Val'," Tina said, then let out a long sigh. "Fuck, that was harder than I thought. Can you lay it out on the table so I can read it all over and see if anything needs to be changed?"

"Sure, honey," Eileen replied, then spread the pages out in order before she capped the pen. "More tea, Emlen?"

"Please, Ma. And another one of those little sandwiches. My kids seem to like those."

"You mean, they don't give you acid reflux and it keeps them settled?" Eileen said, a smile spread across her face as she poured more tea for them both and pulled the plate of food closer.

Tina stepped back from the table. "Let's change this piece here." She leaned over and murmured to Eileen as the additions were made, then sighed. "Okay. It looks as good as it's gonna get. I just hope he believes it's me."

Eileen gathered up the pages and folded them together into an envelope. "That signature should do it. Snookie?" A grin as she wrote 'Brian' on the front of the envelope and set it aside before she sat back down.

"It'll go in the jar when Cullen gets out of his meeting with Connor. Thank you, Tina, for everything. I know that was difficult," Emlen said.

"Difficult was seeing Ryan's ghost and Kian's missing legs. Difficult would be anything happening to you and those babies," Tina replied. "Oh, I wanted to ask you something. When JJ died, did you feel the magic rush when it returned? I mean, you being the only Descendant left and all?" Emlen paused mid-sip and furrowed her brow.

"Y'know, I don't know. I've been feeling all off balance with the changes from the twins and the surge we all got in Dublin, I didn't even notice."

"And with you right there, the emotion of the event could have masked the emotional flash you might have had," Eileen said.

"Well, if you got his magic boost, then it might mean your magic is stronger. We can check if your telepathy is stronger by having you reach out further than you have before," Tina suggested. "See if you can reach Amos. He's stationed in the guard shack by the back gate. That's the farthest point on the property right now."

Emlen let out a breath and closed her eyes. ~Amos, can you hear me? If you can, just think your reply.~

Tina giggled, then covered her mouth.

After a few moments, Emlen laughed.

Amos had replied. ~I can hear you, Ma'am. Does this mean you could read my mind anytime?~

"He's worried I can read his mind anytime," Emlen told Tina and Eileen.

~No, I can't any time. But it seems my range has increased. Thank you for answering. I'll send out some coffee and a bowl of Mrs. A's beef stew in a few.~

~That sounds amazing, Ma'am. Thank you. And Teagan is out here with me. We're not allowed to stand outside guard duty solo anymore.~

~Not a problem, Amos. Thanks again.~ "I need to ask Mrs. A to send some of her stew and coffee out to Amos and Teagan in the guard shack," Emlen said.

"So it worked. Congrats," Tina said.

Eileen got to her feet. "I'll go talk to Mrs. A. You want some stew to go with the sandwich?"

"Thanks, that sounds good," Em replied as Eileen left the room. She turned back to Tina "I want to test this, so over the next few days I'll see how far I can reach. Thanks for reminding me."

"Not a problem. I mean, JJ made such a big deal out of how our mom reacted when she felt me die and how he reacted when he felt her die. I was surprised when you didn't say anything about it when he died."

"I think I was more surprised that he was finally dead. Yes, he was my bio dad, but he was never a father to me. James O'Brien and my Grandpa Brewster were always the male parental figures in my life."

"Have...have you seen my mom around?" Tina asked.

"No, I haven't. I was wondering if maybe she crossed over. My mom's been popping in a lot, checking on me and the babies, but she's trying to not be all in my business all the time. I love her, but when she kept showing up in the middle of my private time with Cullen, we had to set some boundaries."

Tina gave a soft snort of laughter. "Yeah, that'd be awkward." Her smile faded and she sighed. "I looked Between for mom and didn't see her. I think I would've felt it if she crossed all the way. I just..."

"You're just worried she'll be upset that you killed JJ. I get it. But from what Connor told us, those letters were pretty specific. None of us were supposed to stay alive."

"She'll understand. We talked about how messed up the Judge made Johnny over the years. She knows it wasn't on her."

"Good. I'd like her to get to meet the twins when they're born. If she wants."

"I think she wants to. I'm excited to be an auntie again."

"Grand-auntie," Emlen teased.

"Oh, shut it, woman. You're so mean," Tina joked back.

Later that afternoon, Cullen put the jar on a shelf in the corner of the library and put the letter inside. The lid was put back on. Emlen, Cullen, and Tina all looked at each other.

"Anyone see anything?" Cullen asked.

"Not me," Tina said.

"Me neither. Open the jar and see if it's still in there?" Emlen suggested.

Cullen lifted the lid. "Well, the letter is gone. Now, we wait. I guess we just check the jar a few times a day to see if something gets sent back."

"Okay, then. How about a movie, Cull?" Emlen said.

"Sure, I think the new superhero movie is on the streaming service. You get the popcorn and drinks, and I'll pull it up?"

"Sounds like a plan," Emlen replied.

"I'll pop back in later," Tina said and faded out.

Emlen took a slow breath. "This is really hard on her. She's watching the men she loved and admired turn into monsters. I don't know if I'd handle it as well as she has been."

"Me neither. She's been amazing through all of this. Even killing JJ was a positive thing in my eyes. That sick fuck would've laughed as we all burned."

"I agree. Okay, I'm going to go get the popcorn. What do you want to drink?" Emlen asked.

"Chocolate milk. Just like you," Cullen said and smiled at her.

"You know me so well," Em said and kissed him before waddling out of the room towards the kitchen.

Chapter Eighteen

Christmas Eve Mass at St. Anthony's was attended by the whole O'Brien clan, including Connor and his lady friend, Brenna. They'd started dating before Thanksgiving but had only decided to get serious a couple of weeks ago. With all of Connor's travel, he'd not made time for a relationship and the family was happy to welcome the musician into the fold. Brenna played harp for the New York Philharmonic, so she had a travel schedule to rival Connor's.

Emlen thought they were adorable together. Brenna had dark hair with red lights and dark green eyes. A few inches shorter than Connor in heels, she moved with the grace of a ballet dancer, a light in her eyes whenever they landed on her man.

They were all staying in the manse for the holiday, and Eileen and Mrs. A had gone all out with the decorations. A tree had been decorated in the family room, formal parlor, and library. Long boughs of green with dark red velvet bows and tiny gold balls decorated door frames and stair railings, wound around with tiny gold strands of lights. Wreaths hung from wide red ribbon and bows on every single window in the whole place with a garland that wrapped the front door archway. The planters on either side of the door boasted small, decorated trees and lights were wound around the columns, garland, trees and the twin wreaths that decorated the double front doors.

After Mass, back at the manse, everyone enjoyed warm spiced cider or hot cocoa and a selection of Mrs. A's cookies before heading to bed. Plans to meet in the family room around ten were greeted with laughter as Cullen warned that next year the twins would be celebrating their first Christmas and likely have them up at the crack of dawn.

The next morning, everyone made their way downstairs in warm, comfortable clothes and settled in the family room. Eileen sat on the floor by the tree and James delivered the presents as she read the tags. Each person opened their gift before the next one was given, so everyone could see each gift. Brenna had bought them each a special ornament, with Cullen and Emlen admiring the delicate figures in wedding attire and "First Christmas Together" and the date below their names. Even Mrs. A got a rolling pin with her name and the date on it.

Emlen had given Cullen, Connor, and James matching bracelets. Paracord and leather, each had 'O'Brien' engraved on the underside of the metal bar while the front of the bar boasted a Celtic shield knot. Eileen had a gold Celtic shield charm for her charm bracelet and Emlen had had a pendant made for herself and Brenna. Cullen had given Em a charm pendant with a charm of a mother holding the hands of two children, so she slid her own pendant on the charm ring.

"I'll wear this always," she whispered to Cullen.

"As I will always wear this," Cullen replied.

Em also had Mira and Patrick put protection charms on the bracelets and pendants, but they couldn't discuss that with

Brenna in the room. Not yet, anyway. Connor hadn't felt it was time to expose all of the family secrets. A delicious brunch had them all gathered in the dining room when the doorbell chimed and James went to answer it. He called for Cullen a few moments later and the two of them carried a huge box into the room.

"This was just delivered for Em. The guards checked it and deemed it safe," James said.

"It's from Susan and Angelica," Cullen said as he handed Emlen a card.

Emlen read it out loud. "Wishing all of you a very happy holiday. We're spending the holiday with our families at Disney in Florida, and we're having a wonderful time. Thank you for the amazing gift. This box has gifts for all of you and then some. Love from all of us, but mostly Susan and Angelica."

She finished reading and looked at Cullen, "What is she talking about?"

Cullen shared a look with Connor, then shrugged.

"Cullen Murphy O'Brien," Emlen said, hands on her hips. "If you don't tell me right now..."

Connor laughed, "Well, you got the Mom-voice down already, sis. Relax. Cullen and I felt that since Susan had been shot on our watch, we owed her. Set up a Disney vacation for a week for them and their whole family."

"And why did you hide this from me? That's wonderful!" Emlen said as she wrapped her arms around Cullen and kissed his cheek.

"Well, it was a lot of money," Cullen muttered.

"I don't care. We have more money than we'll ever spend, or our kids will ever spend. Now, let's open this box," Emlen said.

Cullen pulled out a pocket knife and sliced the box open, folded it back, then looked up at Em. "Want me to hand them out?"

Em rubbed her lower back. "Yes, please. If I bend over to reach into that box, I might end up curled up in it."

Everyone chuckled as Em took her seat and left it to Cullen. There were gifts for everyone, even Brenna. Each item was a hand-knit or crocheted gift. A pair of fingerless gloves, infinity scarf, and soft beret for Brenna in a beautiful green, blue for Eileen, and violet for Emlen. A knit cap and scarf for each of the guys, and then two large boxes with 'baby boy' and 'baby girl' on each one. Emlen opened one and Cullen the other. Each box held several outfits and two thick blankets, booties, caps – a treasure of handmade beauty in a variety of colors.

Emlen wiped tears from her cheeks, then pulled out her phone and dialed Susan. The phone was set on the table and speaker button hit. "Hi, Susan, happy holidays. Thank you so much for the incredibly generous and beautiful gifts," Emlen said.

Everyone called out their thanks and Susan laughed. "You're all very welcome. We made some of the baby things new and some are pieces our grandchildren wore. All washed and packed up and ready for those beautiful twins."

"The blankets are gorgeous. What's the extra yarn pinned to them for?" Eileen asked.

"So they can be personalized when we know the names and date. Just put it aside and when we come visit to meet your children, we'll finish them."

Emlen sniffled and Cullen called out, "Thank you, Susan and Angelica. We're honored and grateful. Have a wonderful rest of your holiday."

"You all enjoy your holiday too. Much love. Bye!" Susan and Angelica called out before they hung up.

Cullen pulled Em close and kissed her cheek. "Love you, Em," he murmured in her ear.

"Love you too, Cull."

Before Brenna and Connor headed back to New York, Brenna treated them to an evening of harp music. Emlen fell asleep against Cullen's shoulder since the harp music did a beautiful job of quieting the twins.

The rest of the month went by fast and soon it was time for Cullen and Em to go to New York for New Year's Eve. They weren't going to go out to Times' Square or anything crazy because Emlen got too uncomfortable on her feet after about ten minutes. They gathered at Connor's townhouse where he'd set up the rooftop garden to be a winter wonderland. Heaters kept the air warm, a fire pit glowed in the center of comfortable chairs and a table held sparkling grape juice in champagne flutes. A feast was set out and the set up on the roof gave them a clear view of the Times' Square ball and fireworks.

Emlen got on Brenna's good side pretty quickly by sharing stories of the brothers and some of the mischief they'd got up to. They all counted down and the couples kissed at midnight. They spent a little more time, enjoying the fireworks and hot cocoa before they all headed down to bed.

Cullen and Emlen cuddled the next morning and talked about how good Brenna was for Connor and how happy they were that he had someone that made him laugh. They all gathered around the table for breakfast, but about ten minutes in, Connor stood up. "Brenna, I have a question for you, but before I ask it, there's something I need to tell you."

Emlen stuffed a bite of cinnamon roll in her mouth so she wouldn't say anything and Cullen arched a brow at his brother, silently asking if he was sure.

Connor gave Cull a nod and turned back to Brenna. "What do you know about magic?" Connor asked her.

"Magic? Um, like magic tricks?" Brenna said.

"No, love. Like real magic," Connor said.

Brenna started to laugh but stopped when she saw Cullen and Emlen's serious expressions. "Wait, you're serious?"

Em nodded. "Yep."

Connor held out his hand, palm up, and let the lightning swirl above his hand. "Magic."

Brenna sucked in a breath, eyes wide. "Shut the front door! That's awesome."

He let the lightning disappear and leaned over to kiss Brenna. "You're awesome." Then Connor dropped to a knee and pulled a small box out of his pocket in a well-known shade of blue. "Brenna Moran, would you do me the honor of becoming my wife?"

Brenna tapped a finger against her lips and looked up at the ceiling, then sighed, "Oh, I suppose I could do that."

Emlen burst into laughter and clapped as Brenna kissed Connor and Cullen cheered.

"Welcome to the family, sis," Emlen told Brenna.

Connor slid a square-cut emerald with diamond band on Brenna's finger and kissed her again.

"It's perfect, Connor. I love you," Brenna told him.

Cullen called Eileen and James so Connor could share the news. Later that afternoon, Cullen and Emlen flew home, leaving the happy couple to celebrate the new year and their new promises together.

Chapter Nineteen

Peter Wolfe was now too weak to sit in his chair. He lay in a hospital bed, attended by private nurses with regular visits by the soldiers in his inner circle. At the moment, he lay while a nurse rubbed lotion on his feet. His gaze was locked on the small shrine he'd had one of his men set up this morning.

Valentine's Day, February fourteenth, Valentina's birthday was when he would buy her favorite gardenias and roses, put out his favorite photos and light candles.

"Nurse, would you get the blue clay jar off the shelf in the parlor and put it on the cabinet over there next to the pictures?" Wolfe asked.

The nurse paused, wiped off her hands on a towel and stepped out of the room. She came back a few moments later with the jar. As she held it in one arm so she could move a few of the photos around to make room, the jar slipped and she almost dropped it. The lid slid off against her chest and she carefully pulled it up and set it on the cabinet before placing the jar down.

"Sir, there's an envelope in here. Do you want it?"

"An envelope?" Wolfe was confused. JJ was dead. How would there be an envelope?

"Yes, sir. Should I take it out?"

"Please, and bring it to me," Wolfe replied.

The nurse set the jar carefully in its spot and put the lid back on, then brought the letter over to Wolfe. When he saw 'Brian' on the front, he almost dropped it. "Open it for me."

The nurse opened the envelope and pulled out the pages. She unfolded them and held them for him to read.

"I can't read it. Please, read it to me?"

The nurse sat on the chair at the side of the bed and cleared her throat before she started reading. "Dearest Brian, Someone is writing this for me because ghosts can't hold pens very well." The nurse paused and looked up at her patient. "Is this a joke?"

"I...uh...what's the signature?"

"Always and forever, Snookie – your Vali girl," the nurse said.

Alarms went off and Wolfe's body jerked and shuddered in the bed. The nurse dropped the letter and grabbed the cart, pulling out a prepared syringe and injecting some into the IV already dripping into his veins. A moment later, the seizure stopped and Wolfe drifted into sleep.

The nurse knew he'd want her to read the letter to him when he woke, so she sat down and read through it. None of it made any logical sense to her, so she folded it back up, slid it into the envelope, and lay it on the bedside table. Right now, her patient needed rest.

Emlen rubbed her lower back and grimaced. The weight and strain had been rough to deal with last month but now it felt like a sack of bowling balls strapped to her stomach. She'd forgotten what her feet looked like and had got tired a while back of having to ask someone to help her with her shoes. Curled on her side, propped with pillows, felt like the only way she could get a deep breath. She had tucked herself in to the corner of her favorite sofa with her e-reader and tried to focus, but the pain throbbed in her back.

Cullen spotted Em through the open door as he came in from outside. He shook the snow free and pulled off his outer gear before he stepped into the room, hands held out to soak up the warmth from the fireplace. "Hey love, I'll come to greet you in a minute. My hands are chilled."

"Hey," Em said. "Thanks. Warm 'em up and you can maybe rub my lower back a little?"

Cullen settled on the sofa beside Em and helped her shift so he could rub her back. Low groans slid from Em's lips as she relaxed over the pillows and cushions, the tension eased for the first time all day.

"Much better," she mumbled.

Cull reached for the bag he'd set next to the sofa and pulled out a small box of handmade chocolates. "Happy Valentine's day, wife. It's our first Valentine's as husband and wife and I know you don't like the holiday, but I wanted to do something to mark the occasion."

"Aww, that's sweet of you. Thank you. Sorry, but I wasn't in any condition to go out and get you something."

"Love, you're carrying my children. That's more than enough. Now, let me help you shift and I'll rub your feet."

Em made a sound between pleasure and pain as she used his help to prop up against the pillows and lay her feet in his lap. She opened the chocolates and read the little card, then picked out his favorite to feed to him. "You rub my feet? I feed you chocolate. We can pretend we're ancient Romans."

Cullen laughed and bit the chocolate as his thumbs dug into the arches of her feet.

Wolfe finally woke up after his episode and saw the letter on his side table. He called the guard over to him and asked him to read the letter out loud.

It took everything within the man to restrain himself, but Wolfe had long ago stopped being Brian Peters. He wished he had his strength just one more time, so he could tear the letter into shreds along with whomever had sent it to him. Tears slid down his withered cheeks, thinking of the cruelty the writer inflicted upon him, pretending to be his sweet angel. Voice cracking with fury, Wolfe pulled the oxygen mask away from his mouth and ordered the day's events to begin.

A monitor had been pulled close to his bed and the man that had once been Brian Peters watched as a series of explosions were triggered.

The guard turned away from the screen in time to see the heart rate monitor flat-line. A hand reached over and silenced the alarm, then tugged the blanket up over Wolfe's face. "Evil fucker. Hope you rot in hell," the guard muttered as he left the room.

Tina had been waiting for the moment she felt Brian connect with the letter. She hadn't expected it to be just before he died. Tina made sure that Em tucked a small gemstone from one of Tina's earrings in the envelope. They'd hoped it would be enough of a belonging to draw Tina to Brian. It had been. Barely.

"Brian," Tina said as she stood next to his bed. She could feel his spirit, still in his body. His heart had stopped moments ago but his brain did not yet register that he was dead. "Brian, stop dicking around. You're dead. Accept it, already."

"No," Brian said as his ghost started to separate from his body. "I didn't get to see the end game."

"Suck it up, sweetcheeks. Your game is ended."

"Who the fuck are you, anyway?" Brian asked.

"Open your eyes and sit up and you'll see." Brian's ghost sat up and swung his legs over the side of the bed. He stared at his hands and moved his limbs, then lifted his gaze and saw Tina, arms crossed, one brow arched as she watched him.

"Welcome to the Dead Zone," Tina teased.

"Valentina," Brian whispered, then pushed to his feet and reached for her. Tina stepped back,

"Woah, buddy. Back off."

"But my love, everything I've done is for you. Revenge against those that killed you!"

Tina leaned in, pointed finger in his face, "You fucking moron," she hissed, "You killed my friends. You killed a lot of innocent people. You got off on the killing. You are not the man I loved."

Brian tried to grab Tina's finger, so she curled it into a fist and slammed it into his chest. He stumbled back and sat on the bed, hand lifted to rub where she hit.

"How can you do that?"

"Moron. We're both ghosts," Tina said.

Brian looked around before his gaze settled back on Tina. "Where's the white light?"

Tina snorted laughter. "Riiight. Like you're going to go to heaven? No. First you go Between. Then you get sorted from there."

"So why are you not sorted?"

"I chose to stay. You, however, don't get that choice."

"Why not? Everything I did, I did out of love for you."

"No, Brian. Everything you did, you did because you got a rush out of it. Power, control, life, death – it was all in your hands, right?"

Brian smiled, "That's right. I did control it all. Today, I took out the last set of leaders. PLEA's UN offices are nothing but smoke and ash."

"No, Brian. Oh, my gods, what did you do?" Tina had a moment of panic, then huffed a breath and grit her teeth. "Fine." She took a deep breath and shouted "Ryan." Ryan appeared beside her and looked at Brian. "Ryan, Brian blew up PLEA UN. I think we've had enough of him, don't you?"

"Yeah, we've had enough," Ryan said and grabbed for Brian. Brian struggled but Ryan just smiled. "Hold on, ya little turd."

Tina grabbed Brian's other arm and they dragged Brian toward the window. The clear glass panes shifted to smoky gray, then black. Tina let go and Ryan shoved Brian towards the blackness. When Brian tried to turn back, Ryan kicked him into the black and watched as Brian's ghost fall into oblivion.

"We've got to get to Emlen. Connor was at the UN offices today," Tina said.

Ryan took her hand and they disappeared, only to reappear in the manse.

Chapter Twenty

"Emlen," Tina started to say and then stopped. "What?"

Emlen was on her hands and knees, gripping the back of the couch, rocking and panting. "I'm...in...labor..." Em gasped out as she looked at Tina. "Did you...get him?"

"He was dead. Ryan shoved him Between. Where's Cullen?"

"I'll go find him," Ryan said.

"Cullen's getting the car and the guards," Eileen said as she came into the room. "How are you doing, Emmy?"

"They're close. Really close," Em said.

Eileen bit her lower lip. "You okay with me taking a look under your skirt, honey?"

"It burns, Ma, like fire," Emlen said, fingers curled tight into the cushions and frame of the sofa. "Should have left the minute my water broke."

"Yeah, well..." Eileen crouched down and lifted the hem of Em's dress. Her eyes went wide and she got to her feet. "Emmy? You're not going to make it to the hospital. Stay where you are and whatever you do, do not push." Eileen raced to the door, yelling at the top of her lungs. "Cullen, get down here. James, call Michaelson next door. I saw his car this morning, so the good doctor is home. Mrs. A? Get clean sheets and towels, hot water, dental floss, and your sharpest scissors. Now, people!"

Cullen slid into the doorway, grabbed the door frame and hurried to Em. He knelt in front of her, behind the couch and gripped her hands. "Hang on to me, baby. I've got you."

Eileen spread towels on the couch and floor, washed her hands in the scalding water and folded Em's dress up over her hips. Em screamed, pushed, and the first baby's head slid out and started to turn.

Tina blinked out of the room for a moment and returned with Camille and Joel, the three of them staying in the hallway.

Emlen yelled again and Camille moved closer. "I'm here, Emmy. You're doing great. Breathe between pushes."

"Mama, it hurts so bad," Em said.

"I know, honey, but you'll forget that soon enough."

"Emmy, one more push and your first baby will be here," Eileen called out, cradling the baby's head as Em cried out and pushed and the sturdy little body slid free into Eileen's hands.

"Your son is here," Eileen said as she handed the baby to Mrs. A and tied off the cord with the dental floss. "Cullen, come cut the cord, son." Eileen handed her son the scissors as he stared at the baby covered in birthing fluids and wrapped in a bath towel.

She nudged Cullen and held up the cord for him to cut, then took the scissors from him as he reached for the babe.

"Go show his Mama and then we'll clean him up. Still have his sister to get here."

Cullen carried the boy over and showed Emlen. "Oh, my. He's gorgeous." she whispered and reached out to touch his face. "Hello, little one. I can't wait to hold...owwww."

Her words ended in a howl of pain as another contraction hit and the first placenta slid free, soon followed by the crowning of their daughter. The second one's birth went a lot faster and it wasn't long before both babies were washed and bundled, Em was cleaned up and all were settled up in the master suite.

Dr. Michaelson had just pronounced them all in perfect health, weighed and measured and recorded the babies' births. "Camille Eileen and Connor James," Em said as she held her daughter to nurse while Cullen cradled their son who had just finished eating. "Okay, Cami, you're done," Em said and settled the baby on her lap. "Cami and CJ. Sound good to you?"

"Sounds perfect. They're perfect. You're perfect," Cullen said. They cuddled together and admired their beautiful children, Em's head on Cull's shoulder. The sound of a throat being cleared brought both their heads up.

"Connor, when did you get in?" Cullen asked.

"Uh, I don't know?" Connor said as he looked around, confused. "Wait, you had the babies?"

"Just a couple of hours ago," Em said. "Meet Camille Eileen and Connor James."

"Cami and CJ," Cullen said.

"They're..." Connor started to say, then he disappeared.

Emlen sucked in a breath and Cullen froze.

Emlen yelled for Tina and Cullen bolted from the bed, racing downstairs to the office.

Tina appeared. "I heard you yell. Are the babies okay?"

Both babies were fussing at the distress their mom was putting out. "The kids are fine. I need you to find Connor. He just appeared, looking confused, then disappeared," Emlen said.

"He's dead?" Tina said.

"I don't know. He didn't act like a regular ghost. He was at the PLEA offices in the UN."

"Oh, shit. I forgot. Brian said he blew up the UN. I thought he was just being a dick before we tossed him Between. I meant to say something but when I got here, you were kinda having babies coming out of your..."

"Yeah, yeah, I know, I was there. Can you find Connor? Find out if he's alive?" Emlen's voice cracked and she rested a hand on her son. "I want CJ to know his uncle's touch on this side of the veil."

"I'll do my best, Em," Tina said and disappeared.

Emlen bowed her head over the babies, kissed them and curled her arms around them. "If you two have any power towards luck, please send it your Uncle Connor's way."

Tina found herself in the smoke and ash of the ruins where PLEA's UN office had once stood. "Connor, where are you?" Tina called out. She made her way through the chaos of first responders and dogs, calling out until she heard a voice call back.

"Here. I'm here," Connor said, hand raised through the rubble in ghost form.

Tina rushed over to him. "Hang in there, Connor. Help's coming." Tina stuck her head through the debris to see Connor's situation, she saw that he was in a pocket created where two beams crossed and held a panel up to give him air and kept his body from being crushed. "Hang in there, Connor. I'll get you help." Tina pulled back out and looked around, getting landmarks so she could tell them how to find him. She popped back to Boston and spotted Scatha. "Hey Scatha, need to tell Cullen where Connor is. Can you translate?"

~Of course. What can you tell me?~

"He's in a pocket of rubble on floor two, between a storage closet hanging open that has blue paint on the inside of the door and a huge pillar that someone spray painted a red C on."

~I'll tell Cullen, he can relay it to the PLEA folks helping search. Come with me.~

Tina followed the raven into the command center and listened as he relayed the information. "Scatha, tell him that Connor is still alive but I don't know how long that will be the case," Tina said.

~Cullen, Miss Tina says that Connor is still alive but she doesn't know for how long. He is gravely injured.~

Cullen yelled into the microphone. "He's on the second floor, next to a column with a C on it, which means you already called it cleared! Get back up there and get my brother."

It took about twenty minutes before they got the call that they'd found Connor and were working on getting him out. Another thirty minutes and they got the all clear that he was being transported to the hospital.

Tina went up to Emlen and woke her up to let her know that Connor was alive and rescued.

"Oh, thank you, Tina," Em said as she tugged her into a hug. "Thank you so much. You saved us all. Imagine if Connor was killed the day the twins were born."

"It's also my birthday," Tina said. "Valentine's Day, which is why I was named Valentina."

"How old, Tina?"

"Older than fifty and younger than sixty," Tina laughed.

"Well, happy birthday, Auntie. Thank you again. I love you."

"I love you, too, Emlen. Go ahead and get some rest. I'll hang out and watch the kids and wake you if they fuss."

Em burrowed down into the covers and sighed. "Thanks, Tina."

Chapter Twenty-one

Connor had been released a little over two weeks after the explosion, but he needed rehab and care, so Cullen had him flown back to Boston and they set up a room for him in the manse. Brenna flew back with him and had canceled her Philharmonic engagements until he could be up and around once more. Both legs in casts, bandages in various places, and issues with vertigo that were predicted to clear up once he'd had time to heal, kept Connor propped in a recliner or in bed.

At the moment, he had settled in the recliner and cradled his namesake in one arm, a bright green stuffed dragon in his other hand. Zooming the dragon around while CJ tracked it and waved his fists made Brenna laugh.

Em sat beside them with Cami asleep in the swath of fabric tied around her torso. "I wish you'd let me hire the planner Edmund and I used. I'm not good at this wedding planning crap," Emlen said.

"But we don't want anyone to know other than you and Cullen until it happens. We want small and under the radar," Connor replied.

"I'm fine with being on stage with a hundred other musicians, but I am not so good with being under the spotlight on my own," Brenna said.

"Well, you wouldn't be on your own. Connor would be there, too," Emlen said. "It's going to be a circus, either way, Brenna. The ceremony can be small and intimate, but we'll have to have at least one reception for all of the people I have to play nice with on a regular basis."

Brenna sighed, "I know. But the wedding day itself, that can be kept small and comfortable, right?"

"Yes," Emlen said. "You've got about twenty-five from your family and between blood and chosen family, we've got about forty or so. We can do that at St. Anthony's and then the reception here. With the makeshift command center moved out of the ballroom, there's plenty of room."

"Where'd they move it to?" Connor asked.

"They built out part of the storage in the underground and put it there. Apparently, the cooler temperatures are better for the systems," Em said.

CJ started to fuss and Brenna reached for him. "Oh, someone needs a change. I'll go do it, Em. You stay here and let Cami sleep."

"Thanks, Brenna," Em said and watched her leave before her attention was on Connor. "Okay, time to talk about the thing we've been avoiding. Your ghost or spirit or whatever, showed up here. Scared the everlovin' crap out of Cullen and me. Did the doctor's say whether you'd actually died or not?"

"They said I had been slipping in and out of consciousness and had been on the border of a coma. Maybe that's what happened?"

"I did read that coma patients could spirit walk if they were focused enough," Emlen said, then reached out to squeeze his hand. "I'm just glad you're here. Now, you sure you want to get married before you're able to walk unaided?"

"Yes. I get the plaster off and the braces on to help with therapy two days before St. Pat's. I know I'll need a walker and a chair, but I can stand with a walker and Cullen's support and use the chair the rest of the day. I'm done waiting. Brenna's done waiting. We want to start our lives together before something else threatens to take it away."

"As you wish," Emlen smiled. "Now to see if Edmund and Patrick can make it down for your nuptials. They said they'd do their best. Mira will be here in a few days, so she can stay over and the rest of the gang will show up the day before the ceremony."

"We'll do the 'everyone else' reception in June or July when I can actually dance with my bride. The best of both worlds, eh?"

"Definitely," Emlen said before she shifted Cami in the sling. "I can't believe they're here, sometimes," she whispered. "I'll be doing something else and suddenly it hits me that I'm a Mom."

Connor cleared his throat and glanced at the doorway before his gaze returned to Em. "Give it about seven and a half months, and I'll be a dad."

"Connor, that's fantastic," Em said, tone kept low so as not to wake Cami. "Our kids will be close in age, like you and Cullen. Did you tell your folks yet?"

"No, we were going to tell everyone tonight, but I had to share with my sis, y'know?"

Em leaned over and kissed his cheek. "Congrats, big brother. I need to go get CJ, it's almost feeding time. Don't worry about the wedding, everything will be perfect."

Dinner that night was decidedly celebratory with the wedding plans finalized and the impending addition to the family being announced. The daily routine of the house settled into a pattern with the twins' schedule and health care professionals in and out.

PLEA rented a new office space in New York city while the debris was cleared and rebuilding at the UN had begun. Their resources had focused on taking down any last remnants of Wolfe's organization, but it seemed to have crumbled once the money dried up.

Thomas and Evelyn were at the NY townhouse for the foreseeable future while Connor and Cullen worked from Boston. Mira arrived and once her bodyguards had helped put her bags in the guest room, she didn't want to rest but to see the twins right away.

Emlen brought her into the nursery and over to the crib where they both lay together. "Mira? This is Connor James, or CJ, and Camille Eileen, or Cami. Kids? This is your Auntie Mira and godmother to one of you."

"Oh, Em, they're beautiful," Mira whispered as she leaned over the crib. Bright blue eyes peered up at her from both babies as they examined this new person. "Hello, CJ and Cami. It's truly an honor to meet you." Mira's hand reached down to them and each twin grabbed one of her fingers.

A soft gasp from Mira had Em concerned. She stepped close to the older woman in case she got unsteady before she asked, "What's wrong, Mira?"

"Nothing's wrong," Mira smiled, eyes shining as she looked up at Em. "Nothing at all is wrong. You have two healthy, perfectly un-cursed Descendants here."

Emlen hugged Mira, then pulled back and wiped at her eyes. "I'd hoped. I mean, hell, only took a thousand years before someone figured it out—but you did it, Mira. Thank you, from the bottom of all of our hearts." Em sniffed and then laughed. "I have to call Aoife and her grandmother and tell them it worked."

She darted out of the room to make the call while Mira stood over the crib. "I predict great things from you two and the rest of your family to come. Grow in love and light, little ones."

Chapter Twenty-two

Epilogue

Ten months later CJ and Cami sat in the play area, using telekinesis to build a tower with their blocks. Cassidy, Brenna and Connor's son, was in a bouncy seat near them, cooing at the brightly colored blocks as they swirled nearby. Nana Camille sat in the fenced area with the twins and handed them blocks from the box as they used up the ones already out and Joel clapped whenever they got one placed just so.

Emlen stepped into the room and smiled at the scene before her. "How's everyone doing?"

"Mumma," Cami squealed and held up her arms.

Camille scooped up her granddaughter and handed her to Em, then paused. "I think she needs a change. CJ got changed a few minutes ago, thanks to Joel."

Emlen took her daughter and went to the changing table area and took care of things. "I can't tell you how wonderful it is that the little ones can see and interact with you. I just wish Simone could have spent more time with us."

"Well, she left that message in that box for you. At least you know and aren't wondering any longer," Joel said.

"True. It helped Tina too. That, and the amulets Patrick and Mira came up with that allow Brenna and Connor to see and hear you all. Now Tina can go work with Connor and Cullen and she loves what she's doing," Em said.

"I can't imagine how Simone felt, sacrificing her eternal peace to make sure her son's ghost couldn't continue to spread evil in the world," Camille said.

"I feel bad that I didn't notice him lurking around," Em said, setting little Cami back in the play area.

"And we feel bad that we didn't see him either," Joel said. "But Simone luring him into the Between was both brave and loving. She may be in the Between for a while, but Jackson will be sent into the dark and she will go into the light. That's how these things work."

"I really wanted her to get to meet her grandchildren, though. I know, it's selfish. I'm blessed that you two and Tina get to know them – and that they get to know you."

Camille rose and moved to hug her daughter. "And we're blessed that we get to be part of their lives."

The fluttery ends of Camille's sweater dangled near Cassidy and he reached up to grab at the soft cloth.

Joel called out, "Ladies, look at Cassidy."

Emlen's eyes went wide as she realized Cassidy could see the ghost. "Well, that's new. He's not a Descendant."

"No, but both of his parents are Bloodlines. Times are changing, Em. Maybe for the better," Joel said.

"Right. Finding out that Aoife's grandmother, Cathleen, was Brenna's mother's aunt, now that made things interesting. Small world, eh?" Em said.

"Very small world. And did you see Aoife and Kian at the second reception? He dances pretty well with those prosthetics of his. Technology is amazing," Joel said. "I'm also glad that he's going to stay in Dublin and help rebuild PLEA there." Joel winked and added, "I'm sure Aoife has a lot to do with that decision."

"Wasn't that a beautiful wedding? I loved the Irish step dancers at the first reception," Camille said. "And the second reception this autumn just after Cassidy was born was so much fun."

Em got a bottle of water out of the mini fridge and sat next to Joel. "So, do you know what the rules are for having ghost godparents?"

"I don't know, why?" Joel asked.

Em rested a hand on her belly. "Because we're going to need another set of godparents in about eight months."

Joel hugged her tight. "That's wonderful news. Congratulations," he whispered to her. "More magic in the world is a good thing."

Camille cupped Emlen's cheek and looked into her eyes. "Are you sure you're ready for more?"

Em smiled at her mother. "I'm ready, as is Cullen. We want a big family to love and support each other. Besides, it just adds more magic to the world, right?"

"More magic, yes. I couldn't have wished for a better life for you." Camille said.

"I remember before I could see you, that all I wished for was to know if you were proud of me," Em told her mother.

Camille kissed her daughter's cheeks. "I'm very proud of you. You know they say the best revenge is a life lived well? Your life is being lived well, my daughter."

THE END

Want more? Check out the first book in a new series by T.K. Eldridge - Partners in Crime Supernatural Mysteries, Dead & Buried - https://books2read.com/DeadBuried

Detectives Kennedy and Donovan were partners for years. Then one of them died.

And yet, they're still partners.

Kennedy has to solve Donovan's death while his partner's ghost helps him. Sort of.

How do you explain where you got the tips?

How do you avoid showing them that you're speaking to thin air and no, you haven't lost your mind?

Kennedy has to hide how he's figuring it all out so he can keep his badge and solve the murder - before he ends up dead and buried too.

Chapter Twenty-three

Dead & Buried Sample

Prologue

Being ignored or shunned was not something they were used to. Doting parents, sycophant friends, they all hung on their every word. The best schools, the best clothes, the best trainers, no expense had been spared. When someone grows up with every wish granted, every desire fulfilled, what more could they strive towards?

Oh, they knew they should be grateful. Charitable, even. Instead, they had decided that it was time to take the next step. No more being under parental control, no more answering to every demand of mother or father – it was time to show them just what they'd created.

Thumbs danced across the screen, and the text was sent. A reply came back moments later. *"Target acquired."*

One by one, they'd all come tumbling down. It was only fair. What else was a person supposed to do for family, if not take up their battles when they could no longer fight?

Chapter One

Jameson Kennedy made his way around the tangled crowd of vehicles and people. A flash of his badge and he ducked under the yellow tape, steeling himself for the sight of yet another body. The sideways looks he was getting from the other cops and techs made the hairs on the back of his neck stand up. Donovan had been his partner for all eight years of his detective career. They knew each other's families, their kids went to school together, his ex-wife and Donovan's wife were friends – they were as close as brothers. If this really was Donovan lying in the mud at the side of the road, he had to keep it together. He couldn't break down in front of everyone.

Finally the last row of people parted, and he stepped close enough to see the body.

He couldn't stop the hard intake of breath. It felt like someone had just punched him in the chest. Mud splattered the sweatshirt and jeans of the figure before him, but he recognized the college logo and the splash of green paint he'd put on the faded blue cloth just last week. The face was mud-splattered, battered and bloody, but he knew it well. He tried to speak, but his voice cracked, so he cleared his throat and said, "Yes, that is Michael Donovan."

"Positive identification made of the victim as Michael Donovan, detective second grade, Harbor PD," the coroner said as he moved back to allow his assistants to finish bagging Donovan's hands and putting his body into the bag.

"Sorry for your loss, Kennedy," Dr. Finney said as he passed him.

Crime makes a mark. It leaves a scar that resonates in the atmosphere of the place where it happened. Jameson Kennedy knew he would never pass this place again without feeling the pain of Donovan's loss.

"I want to do the notification," Kennedy said.

"Take Edgars with you," Sergeant Simmons replied.

"Whatever," Kennedy muttered as he headed back to his car.

Jerry Edgars, new to the squad, was standing beside the car when Kennedy got there.

"Sarge called you?" Kennedy asked.

"Yes, sir. I'm sorry for your loss," Edgars replied.

"Just stay quiet and get in. I know Katherine Donovan, so let me talk, okay?"

"Understood."

They were both silent as Kennedy drove them the half mile to Donovan's house and pulled up out front.

"I don't suppose you'd stay in the car?" Kennedy asked Edgars.

"Sarge said I was to stay with you as a witness in case she said something," Edgars replied.

Rage surged, but he swallowed it down. The knee-jerk reaction to protect his partner and his partner's family had to be kept in check. He had to behave as if this were any other notification for any other case. Silence seemed his best choice, so Kennedy gave Edgars a nod and got out of the car.

He walked across the grass front lawn and up to the door. The simple brick two-story with a front porch that wrapped around one side and a fenced-in backyard was just like any other suburban home. He knocked on the door and waited as Katie opened it and gave him a smile.

"Hey, Jamie. Mike went to the store, but he should be back any minute," Katie said. "Want to come in for a coffee?"

"Hi, Katie. This is Detective Edgars. We need to speak with you. The kids at school?" Kennedy said.

"Jamie, what's wrong? Yes, the kids are at school."

Jamie took her hands in his and looked her in the eyes. "Katie, I just came from a crime scene. Someone killed Mike."

"No, he's just at the store. He called and asked if the store brand was fine. He should be home any moment."

"I had to identify his body, Katie."

That's when she started to sob and leaned into Kennedy's chest. He walked her over to the couch and sat her down, still holding her for the moment. "Let me call Elise to come be with you, okay? She can get the kids and come be here."

Katie nodded and sniffled, then got to her feet. "Tissues. I'll be right back."

They watched her go into the half-bath under the stairs, heard the water turn on, then they heard a howl of such pain it caused both men to flinch. Edgars took a step towards the sound and Kennedy shook his head. "Let her get it out and pull herself together. She's been a cop's wife for fifteen years, she'll be okay. I need to call my ex."

Kennedy pulled out his phone and hit the button to dial.

"I don't need your shit right now, Jamie," the voice said, and Kennedy sighed.

"Elise, I'm calling for Katie. Mike was killed, and I identified his body about half an hour ago. Can you get her kids at school and come be with her? She's going to need you."

"*Oh, fuck,*" Elise said. *"I'll get them and be there in thirty minutes. Are you staying with her until I get there?"*

"I'm not leaving her alone. Edgars and I are here right now."

"*On my way,*" and the call disconnected.

Get your FREE copy of Dead & Buried now! https://books2read.com/DeadBuried

About the Author

T.K. Eldridge retired from a career in Intelligence for the US Gov't to write. The experiences from then are now being used to feed the muse for paranormal romance, mysteries, supernatural, and urban fantasy stories. When they're not writing, they are enjoying life in the Blue Ridge mountains of western North Carolina. Two dogs, a garden, a craft hobby and a love of Celtic Traditional music keep them from spending too much time at the computer.

You can connect with them on:
https://tkeldridge.com
https://tkeldridge.com/newsletter
https://www.bookbub.com/profile/t-k-eldridge

CPSIA information can be obtained
at www.ICGtesting.com
Printed in the USA
BVHW031959120323
660268BV00016B/277